I0779391

Treasure in Paradise: The Bolton Chronicles

Book 1: The Reluctant Adventurer

By Alan Van Ormer

ISBN-13: 978-1-962168-16-8

Chapter 1

Wil Bolton perched himself on a bench right outside of one of Deadwood's casinos and watched jaded tourists shuffling to their gambling destination while children's eyes lit up at the festivities on Main Street.

Wil, who recently turned twenty-five, had lived in the Deadwood area for the past two years after graduating from Frostburg State University in Maryland. He currently worked for the Black Hills National Forest Service as a go-to guy who the forest-service director turned to for tracking down wild animals or rescuing lost hikers.

He stared at the cobblestones that outlined Deadwood's historic Main Street. In the early 1990s, Deadwood's restoration of the street took two years. It stemmed from a fire that destroyed three buildings along Main Street in 1987. Then in 1988 a statewide vote legalized limited stakes-gaming operations, and the gaming industry had grown ever since. Just recently the city planners turned a slime plant near Water Street into a facility for gambling, concerts, and other types of entertainment.

"You look like you're concentrating on the

cobblestone streets."

Wil peered up at a light brown-haired gal with bright green eyes and a smile radiating her pearly white teeth. She wore a light green strapless miniskirt which featured her womanly attributes.

"You caught me trying to count how many cobblestone bricks are used to make a row."

She laughed. "How many are there?"

Wil grinned. "I'm up to thirty-three."

She laughed once more and stuck out her hand. "I'm Kelsey Lawrence."

He shook it. "Nice to meet you, Kelsey Lawrence. I'm Wil Bolton."

"Are you a tourist?"

"Nope," he said. "I moved to the Black Hills two years ago. Yourself?"

"I'm visiting from Chicago with some friends who wanted to play tourist —hiking, horseback riding, and trying their luck at gambling in the Black Hills casino."

"You've been busy."

She grinned. "The only thing we've done is gamble since we arrived here last night. This is what we've planned this week."

"No luck gambling?"

"Nope. I lost fifty bucks in five minutes."

"Ten bucks a minute. Pretty bad odds even in Deadwood."

She frowned. "You're a little sarcastic, aren't you?"

"Sorry, I just hear so many stories about people losing money in the casinos, it always makes me wonder why they continue to do it."

"If you don't gamble, why are you sitting out here

on a bench?"

He pointed at something behind her, and Kelsey turned to look. "What?"

"Watch."

She jumped when the guns went off. "Wow, what is happening?"

"It's a shootout during the Trial of Jack McCall that happens most nights during the summer. McCall was the guy who murdered Sheriff Wild Bill Hickok while he was playing poker."

"I remember reading about that."

Wil looked down at his cell phone vibrating. "Sorry, I have to go. Nice to meet you." He jumped up and hurried toward the Days of 76 Campground to wait for Bailey Blue to land the chopper that would take him to his destination. As soon as it landed, Wil climbed onto the chopper and took a seat next to Caleb Streeter

The paramedic turned to Wil. "Three hikers didn't come down from the Crows Nest Creek area before dark, and they're lost, although they were able to send a message to local authorities."

Bailey lifted the chopper into the air, and they raced toward Crows Nest Creek which was more than seven thousand feet in the air. Bailey and Caleb were good friends with Wil, and all worked for the Black Hills National Forest Service in some capacity.

"Do you know anything about the three?" Wil asked.

"Two guys and a gal who love to hike. They've always wanted to climb this area and finally got the chance. The problem is they didn't take into consideration the time of day."

"I think I see something," Caleb said.

Sure enough, there was a light shining from a group of rocks. Bailey flew as close as he could to see what was happening. They heard someone hollering, "Over here."

When they hovered over the three hikers, a female waved at them. "Thank you for coming for us. Gabriel broke his leg, and we can't move him," the lady hollered.

"Get as close as you can, Bailey, and I'll swing down to see what I can do," Wil said.

Caleb helped Wil hook onto a line, then Wil slid down toward the rocks. The gal and guy helped bring him to the ledge.

"How bad is it?" Wil asked.

"I'm not sure," the woman said. "He's losing a lot of blood."

Wil made a quick check of the leg and peered up at the other two. "We have to get him to a hospital pronto."

"Will he be okay?" the guy asked.

"I don't know because it's dark out, but my first inclination is that it's pretty bad. Here, help me attach him to this sling so they can haul him up. We'll have to hoof it out of here."

"What? How?" the gal asked.

Wil fastened the man to the rope. "We have to transport him to the hospital as quick as possible, meaning there won't be time to haul all four of us up. We'll be okay." When he was ready, Wil tugged on the rope, and they pulled him up. Once the guy was on the helicopter, Wil waved telling them to go.

Just like that the chopper sped toward Rapid City Monument Hospital.

Wil turned back to the others. "Let's get you back to safety. Follow the path I take and don't deviate, or I won't be able to do anything to help you."

The trio started down the hill slowly. After thirty minutes, Wil stopped them to take a break.

"Thanks for saving us. My name is Misty Swenson, and this is my brother, Jerome. Gabriel is a good friend of ours. We love to hike, but we kind of misjudged the time and the height."

"It happens to hikers," Wil said.

"How can you be so calm?" Jerome asked. "I'm scared out of my—"

"It wouldn't help you two if I was scared, so I try to stay as calm as possible. It helps that I've been along many of these trails in the past."

"Is that what you do—guide people?" he asked.

"Sometimes. I work for the forest service assisting in firefighting, tracking down large animals, and guiding snowmobilers, hikers, and others."

"Sounds like a wonderful job," Misty said.

"Where are you guys from?"

Misty tried to catch her breath. "Newcastle, Wyoming."

"Not too far from home."

"Nope. It was an enjoyable hike until about a few hours ago, then Gabriel slipped, and we heard his leg snap. I hope he's okay."

"Caleb will do some doctoring of his leg en route to the hospital. He's our emergency medical responder on the chopper."

"How many were on the chopper?" Jerome asked.

"Normally three, but tonight a deputy sheriff joined us. I'm sure he'll have some questions for you when you get back."

"Like what?" Jerome asked.

Wil stood and stared at the guy. "If you didn't do anything wrong, you'll have nothing to worry about. Let's move."

They traveled another forty-five minutes until they came up to a landslide that had cut a hole in the side of the path. They couldn't jump across, so he had to devise another plan. Wil took some rope out of his backpack, swung it over, and hooked it to a rock. He pulled on it to make sure it was secure and then slid across with his hands and legs.

Once to the other side. he looked back at the two. "You guys are hikers, so this won't be as tough as you think. I'm not asking you to do what I just did, but I'll swing the rope back to you. Attach it around your waist, and I'll pull you across."

"Are you crazy?" Jerome asked.

"I can't think of any other way to get you across."

"Throw the rope to me," Misty said.

Wil did and she hooked it around her waist. "I'll pull you across slowly. Just try to hold onto the rock ledge the best you can, and don't struggle. If you should slip, I'll drag you back. Are you ready?"

She nodded and grabbed the rock ledge. Wil slowly pulled her across. When she reached him, she grabbed onto his neck and held on tight. Peering into his eyes, she whispered, "Thank you so much."

"Hey, what about me?"

Wil unhooked the rope and threw it back to her brother. He tightened it around his waist and grabbed onto the rock ledge. Wil started to pull him over, but he slipped and became frantic as he dangled in the air.

"Calm down," Wil hollered. "If you don't, we'll be fighting each other trying to pull you over here."

Jerome continued screaming making it worse. Wil struggled to hold onto him, and Misty helped pull him in. It was rough, but they finally saved the guy's life.

"What were you thinking, Jerome?" Misty asked. "Why didn't you listen to what Wil had to say?"

"I was scared."

Misty held her brother. "You're okay now."

Wil slid down a bit aways from the ledge. "We'll take a break here for fifteen minutes."

Once Jerome was settled, Misty slid down next to Wil. "Thank you so much for getting my brother across. We probably shouldn't have brought him along because this was his first hike."

Wil peered back at Jerome who had his eyes closed. "What's with you and your brother?"

"Normal brother, sister relationship, I guess. He's eighteen, and I'm twenty-two. We've been close throughout. Mom and Dad haven't been the best parents, so that's why we stick together."

"What do you do?"

"I'm a bank teller and enjoy visiting with the customers. As you probably realize, everyone knows everyone in Newcastle."

Wil nodded. "And your brother?"

"In between jobs. He's worked in construction but likes to drink a bit too much, and he misses too much time because of hangovers. We live together in Newcastle, but at times I'm still a babysitter for an eighteen-year-old."

"I'm sorry to hear that."

"Don't be. I love my brother and hope he can grow

up soon. What about you? Do you have a family?"

Wil shook his head. "My folks died in a car accident about five years ago. I have one sister, but she left South Dakota a long time ago. She and her husband have three children and are enjoying life in Washington. I'm happy for them."

"Why do you stay here?"

Wil thought for a moment. "I'm really not sure. I do enjoy my work because I'm outdoors most of the time, and I do have some wonderful friends."

"How often do you rescue people?"

"More than you'd believe. It seems at least once a week a hiker or snowmobiler is lost or has an accident. Then there are the fires in the forest."

"You're also a firefighter?"

"I'm not certified per se, but when you work for the national forest, you do a bit of everything. I have dropped down into the middle of fires to rescue people and animals."

"Animals?"

"Yep. They're just as scared as humans at times."

"Fascinating job you have. No wonder you don't want to leave."

Wil stood up. "Wake up your little brother, and let's get out of these hills before the sun comes up."

The three made it to a forest-service station around three in the morning. Waiting for them were the deputy sheriff and Bailey.

"You finally decided to join us." Bailey grinned.

Wil nodded. "Here they are, Deputy. Unless you need something from me, I'm going home to sleep for a week."

Chapter 2

The first person Wil saw when he arrived at work on Monday morning was Amanda Schultz who was sitting at her reception desk. She was not only the forest-service administration assistant but also a close friend of his.

"How are you feeling?" Amanda asked.

"I'm fine. Did you have a wonderful weekend?"

"I surely did."

"So did I."

Amanda laughed. "Go ahead and tell yourself that. Everyone knows you spent the weekend by yourself. Anyway, the boss wants to talk to you."

"Thanks." Wil walked to Hampton's office and stood by the door. The boss was on the phone but waved him in.

"Have a seat," he mouthed.

Wil did just that.

Once he was off the phone, Hampton peered at Wil. "I have a group of people who are interested in taking one of the hiking trails near Cement Ridge Lookout. I want you to guide them up there. They'll be waiting for you shortly."

An hour later Wil pulled into a parking lot just outside of Spearfish Canyon. Waiting for him were three gals and two guys. One of them was Kelsey Lawrence, the girl he'd met on Main Street. He climbed out of his pickup, and she waved at him as he walked over.

"Did you make it to your destination?" she asked.

"I did. Now I'm the one who's going to guide you along the trail."

"They said you were the best guide in the area," said a guy just a bit shorter than Wil's six-one height. He reached out his hand and shook Wil's. "I'm Clinton Sadler, and it seems you know Kelsey already. Also with us are Lisa Horner, Alexis Rider, and JJ Blanch."

Wil took a deep breath. "The vehicle you have won't make it to where we're going, so a couple of you will have to climb into the back of the pickup, and a couple can sit in front."

"I call shotgun," Alexis said.

Kelsey crawled between Wil and Alexis, and the others climbed in the back.

Wil took Road 134 toward Iron Creek Lake, telling them about the area as he drove. "During the winter it's a very slow drive because the lake is usually frozen. Even during the summer, it's a tough climb up to the lookout." He stopped near the lake and climbed out of the vehicle. "You can pitch your tents here, and once you're ready, we'll head up to Cement Ridge Lookout for lunch."

Once they had set up their tents, Wil led the climb

up to Cement Ridge Lookout. They walked for about fifteen minutes when Wil stopped for a moment to have a drink of water. They followed his lead.

"We're in Wyoming now. Cement Ridge Lookout is not too far away."

As they walked, Wil explained to them about the peak. "It's over sixty-six hundred feet and the tallest peak in the Wyoming area of the Black Hills. Much of the time, it is hard to reach it during the winter. The weather wasn't that bad this winter." As they made their way, Wil explained that Cement Ridge is a mountain ridge that has an old fire lookout at the north end of the ridge. "As you've noticed the ridge is covered in thick forest. An off-trail hike up the summit is crazy hard."

They started the climb up to Cement Ridge. "The area is rich in something called Minnekahta limestone. The limestone is used to manufacture cement."

Wil stalled the group for a few minutes to take a breather. They all found some rocks and timber to sit on. "A log cabin was constructed on the summit in the early 1900s followed by a two-story wooden tower in the early 1920s. The summit wasn't accessible until 1927 when a ranger brought his family up to the summit in a Model T Ford." They began the climb once more. "Take it easy. The rocks do make it slippery at times. Most of the broken trees you see on the peak were the result of a tornado during the early 1990s."

Thirty minutes later they made it to the top.

Wil grinned at them. "I should tell you the mountain is on the list of Wyoming's one hundred most remote peaks. People get lost because the roads are minimally marked. Let's take a lunch break." He sat down and munched on a sandwich and chips.

Kelsey came and sat down next to him. "This is beautiful out here. Thank you for bringing us up here and making it so easy. You're much more than a bum sitting on a bench on Deadwood's Main Street."

Wil didn't respond; he just ate and viewed the scenery. He pointed to an animal a couple of hundred yards away. "See the coyote?"

Kelsey's eyes followed his finger. "How were you able to see that?"

"You get used to it when you're out in the wild long enough. I figure out how the animals act, the way they walk, and read their footprints to help me decide what they are."

"Will the coyote come this way?"

Wil shook his head. "They're even more scared of us than we are of them. They only attack when they're cornered or hungry." Wil stood up. "Maybe y'all should check out the area before we head back down. Be back in an hour."

They headed back down the trail back to the base camp quicker, making it back by midafternoon. The group switched into swimming suits and jumped into the lake to cool off.

They'd been swimming for an hour when Lisa climbed out and joined Wil sitting on a rock. "You should have joined us. The water's great."

Wil rolled his eyes. "I didn't bring a swimming suit. Besides, this is fun for you. When do you head back to Chicago?"

"On Saturday. How did you know we were from Chicago?"

"I was sitting on a bench on Main Street while you

were gambling, and Kelsey told me."

"You're the guy she was talking about, and she was right—you are cute."

Wil didn't respond. The two sat and watched the others swim. "For the last couple of years, Clinton has tried so hard to connect with Kelsey, but she just pushes him away, and he hasn't figured out why," Lisa said.

"I can tell that. You have to give the guy credit for the effort."

Lisa laughed. "So many guys have tried to hook up with Kelsey, but she's very particular about who she dates. She's engaged to Nolan Gant, and they are getting married in a couple of months. Who knows if she'll go through with it."

"Why do you say that?"

"Because Kelsey is waiting for a guy to sweep her off her feet."

"That could be a tall order because there can't be many of those guys around."

"You're wrong there. All she wants is a guy to steal her heart."

After supper, the group sat around a fire drinking beers. Alexis snuggled into JJ. "This is so beautiful. I can't remember the last time I saw the stars this bright."

Wil nodded. "At night there are times when the stars shine brighter than you could imagine."

Clinton looked at Wil. "Do you spend a lot of nights under the stars, and what's that like?"

"I do. My cabin is located near Nemo and has a grassy area on one side of me and the Black Hills behind me. I think I've seen every type of wild animal roam through there."

"Including a bear?" Lisa asked.

Wil nodded as he sipped his beer. "I was sitting on my porch drinking a cup of coffee one morning when a bear stopped at Box Elder Creek to take a drink. He peered at the cabin for a moment, then darted into the hills behind the cabin."

"Weren't you afraid?" Alexis asked.

"No, because the bear wasn't interested in me; he was more concerned about drinking water. Wild animals are more afraid of humans than humans are of them. I see more mountain lion tracks then I do bear tracks by far." Wil eyed the group. "Why did you decide to come to South Dakota?"

Kelsey quickly answered the question. "We're all good friends from the Chicago area and wanted to see the Black Hills."

"Have you enjoyed yourself?"

"We have," Alexis said. "I'm surprised by all the beauty out here, and there are many more things to see and do than I thought. We would have never gone on a hike like we did today because you just don't do that around Chicago."

The group talked for another hour before they started to drift to their tents. It was around ten when Wil and Kelsey were the only two left. She slid over near him.

"What do you do for a living?" Wil asked.

"I work in clothing and design."

Wil finished sipping his beer. "Interesting field. Are your friends in that field also?"

"No, they do a little bit of everything. Alexis and JJ are into computers, Lisa is an editor for a magazine, and Clinton is a businessman." Kelsey sipped on her beer. "Do you have any other dreams, or are you happy to lead hikers through the Black Hills?"

He stared out into the fire. "I'd like to travel around the world searching for treasures or artifacts, which would make it hard for anyone to handle a guy who's always gone, so I'll probably be a loner." Wil turned to Kelsey. "What other plans do you have while you're here this week?"

"We planned on going to the Badlands. I hear that it's beautiful."

"It is but a different kind of beauty. While the Black Hills have the trees, the Badlands is a bunch of eroding rocks, and during this time of the year, the heat can be unbearable. You'll need plenty of sunscreen and water."

Kelsey laughed. "I'll remember that." She yawned. "I suppose I should crawl into my sleeping bag. Thank you for taking us on this hike today. I enjoyed myself."

The next morning Wil had coffee brewing as the gang woke up. Kelsey came out of her tent wiping the sleep out of her eyes. She stopped in front of him. "I must look like a mess."

Wil handed her a cup of coffee.

"Thank you," she smiled. "Did you sleep well?"

"I did but then I enjoy the outdoors, so it's always comforting for me. Yourself?"

"Yes, I did, and I'm surprised because I've never slept in a sleeping bag before. I'm usually relaxing in hotel rooms, so it's kind of nice going out of my comfort zone once in a while." She sipped on her cup of coffee. "Someday you'll have to show me your cabin. I heard someone say they're surprised the cabin is still standing because of all the work needed to be done, especially the roof."

Wil laughed. "Whoever that person was would be right, but then again I do have a portion of the roof completed but still have more work to do on it."

"Why don't you just hire someone to fix it?"

He grinned at her. "That wouldn't be any fun."

They turned as the others started coming out of their tents. An hour later after they had breakfasted, the group headed down another trail along a creek bed. They had traveled close to an hour when Wil quickly halted them.

"What is it?" Alexis asked, her eyes wide.

"Stay right here. I'll be back." Wil hurried over to the body he had seen by a group of rocks. He bent down and checked his pulse. The guy was still alive but barely. He pulled out his phone and called the forest-service office.

"Hey Wil, how's the trip?" Amanda asked.

"I need help. Found a guy who's barely alive. I haven't checked on what happened, but he needs medical assistance."

"We're on our way."

Wil gave her the coordinates, got off the phone, and started to check him over, finally discovering blood on his back. He peered up at Kelsey who was standing over him.

"Can I do anything to help?"

"He's been shot, and I need to get the bullet out. Can you start a fire?"

"I've never done it, but I'll try to get one going." She scrambled around to grab sticks and twigs as the others hurried over to see what was happening. Wil peered up at the guys. "I need you two to help me turn him gently to his stomach so I can extract the bullet."

The two guys helped him move him over and lay him onto a blanket that Wil had pulled out of his backpack. Kelsey had the fire going, and Wil handed her a knife from his backpack. "Please, sterilize it so I can cut the bullet out."

"Okay."

While she was doing that, Wil gently pulled away his shirt from the blood. Kelsey handed him the knife. He turned to the others. "Please hold him down as tightly as you can, so if he does wake up or jump, I won't paralyze him."

They did as he asked. Wil took a deep breath and made an incision into the wound. Several moments later, he pulled out the bullet and stuck it into a bag. "Kelsey, there's a sewing kit in the backpack. Could you please bring it to me?"

When Kelsey handed him the sewing bag, they watched as Wil gently sewed the wound shut. Fifteen minutes later a chopper flew over them and landed in a flat area. Caleb came running over with a folded-up stretcher. Wil helped him put it together, and the guys gently lifted the man onto the stretcher, carrying him over to the chopper.

Once he was loaded, Bailey said, "A Wyoming deputy is on his way as we speak."

Wil nodded. Bailey lifted the chopper up and headed toward Rapid City. Minutes later a Wyoming deputy sheriff arrived and asked the group a series of questions. Once he was finished, the group headed back down the trail, and Wil drove them to their vehicle.

Kelsey, who was sitting next to him, waited before crawling out to join the others "Despite how it ended, we all had a wonderful time. Thank you." Just as she slid out, she turned back to him. "I saw the photo of a pretty gal in your backpack. What happened to her?"

"She moved on."

Chapter 3

On Tuesday afternoon, Wil drove into Rapid City. When Wil participated in overnight camping trips, the boss usually gave him the next day off. He had decided to go to the chain bookstore and do some reading, maybe even purchase books that deal with treasure hunting. It was late morning when he stepped into the bookstore and started browsing through the magazines.

Wil noticed an archaeology magazine, grabbed it, then bought a mocha, and sat down at a table in the cafeteria area. He was engrossed in the magazine when he heard a voice.

"Wil, what are you reading that has you so fascinated?"

He looked up to see Kelsey standing near the table. "It's about a group who spent five years trying to find an artifact."

"It sounds like that's a long time to find something," Kelsey said. "Do you mind if I join you?"

"Please do. What brings you to a Rapid City bookstore?"

"Well, I love to browse through books and find

something that is totally different from what I do every day with clothes. I'm mostly into adventure and romance, but I see you're into archaeology."

"I've always been fascinated with history and finding treasures."

"Interesting. That must be why you want to travel around the world. He nodded. She stood up. "I'll let you finish your article and do some looking around for books. If you're still here when I'm done, I'll stop back."

"You do that."

Thirty minutes later Kelsey came back and joined him. He peered up at her. "Did you find anything?"

"Yeah, a couple of books." She handed them to him. "Several books on South Dakota. I love learning about other places. In a way I'm sort of like you."

Wil took a deep breath. "I'm finished with this article. Do you want to go for a ride with me?"

"I'd love to."

"Let me purchase these magazines," Wil said.

~

While Wil was buying the two magazines, Kelsey wrapped her arms around her body. She felt like a young gal in love for the first time in her life. At twenty-three she had been with several guys, but Wil Bolton seemed special, even though she had only been with him a couple of times.

Wil and Kelsey climbed into his pickup truck, and he drove toward downtown Rapid City. He took a winding road up to a place called Dinosaur Park.

Kelsey peered at the statues of dinosaurs as they drove into the parking lot. "Wow, this is cool. I've never heard of this place."

Wil stopped his truck. "Dinosaur Park is one of the favorite stops for those with small children in the Black Hills. The project took place in 1936, and the property has been placed on the National Register of Historic Places."

The two started up the many stone steps leading to the top where there were more dinosaur statues. Once at the top, Wil took Kelsey's hand and pulled her to the highest spot where they could see the city skyline. "Wow, this is so cool," she said.

"This is one of the spots I go to when I just want to get away from everything. I'll sit up here and stare down at the skyline of Rapid City and think about what's happening in my life."

The two walked over to a group of rocks and sat down. "Why are we here?" she asked.

"I really don't know other than it's a beautiful spot, and I wanted to show you the place."

"Thank you."

They were both quiet for a few minutes. Wil finally broke the silence. "Lydia and I used to spend a lot of time up here."

"When did you two meet?" Kelsey asked.

"Two years ago, when I first arrived in South Dakota. We had dated for about six months. She had just finished her law degree, and I had just arrived from Maryland for my job."

"If I'm not prying, what happened to the two of you?"

Wil peered out into the Rapid City skyline. "She was driving home from work one night, it was snowing, and the roads were slippery. Near Central City she lost control of the car, slid into a hill, and was dead on impact."

She touched his arm. "I'm so sorry, Wil."

"It's been a couple of years now, and I'm starting to get over it, but it has taken time."

Kelsey didn't respond, but she kept her hand on his arm.

He switched subjects. "Why aren't you with all of your friends?"

"They wanted to do some more gambling today, and I didn't want any part of that. One time is enough, so I decided to take a trip to Rapid City, check out the bookstore, stroll through the mall for clothes, and eat a taco. They're a little bit behind the times in fashion here in Rapid City."

Wil laughed. "I can imagine. How about joining me tonight? We can barbecue some brats, and you can check out my cabin."

She grinned. "That's the best offer I've had all day."

"You can turn your rental car in here in Rapid City, and I'll drive you back to your hotel in Deadwood."

"Are you sure that's okay?"

"Yep."

As they traveled down Nemo Road, Kelsey asked, "what made you decide to live out here in the sticks?"

"It's quiet and peaceful. Lots of wild animals roam around and like to talk during the night."

"How do you sleep?"

"You get used to it. I've never been afraid."

It was four-thirty when Wil pulled his pickup in front of a cabin. He climbed out and opened the door for her.

"Thank you," she said.

"It's not much, but it suits me fine."

Kelsey stared at the outside of the log cabin and its rustic look. "It's kind of cool really."

Wil walked toward the front door, and she followed him. He opened it and she walked through. It was a small cabin with three rooms that included two bedrooms. She pointed up above. "That's cool—eight chandelier lights hanging from a piece of wood."

"Correct."

"The kitchen sure doesn't look large."

Wil ran his fingers through his hair. "It suits me just fine."

She peered up at him. "It's kind of cozy."

"Thanks. Would you like to go for a hike with me before we eat?"

"I'd love to. Am I dressed appropriately?"

Wil nodded. "Sandals will work fine because I'll keep us away from rattlesnakes and poison ivy."

"That would be nice," Kelsey laughed.

The two spent the next hour hiking up a trail behind the cabin. Once at the top, Wil sat down on a rock and pulled her up next to him. She surveyed the area—the Black Hills in the distance.

"This is beautiful."

"I crawl up here once in a while to get away from the world because of its tranquility."

"I can see why."

The two enjoyed the scenery. Finally, Kelsey gazed up at Wil. "Why did you ask me to join you tonight?"

"I'm surprised you said yes."

"I am very particular about the guys I hang out with, but there is something about you I just can't figure out. I just wanted to find out more about you."

"By the end of the week, you'll be traveling back to Chicago, and we'll probably never see each other again."

"Maybe. Or maybe we'll see a lot more of each other than you'd believe."

He jumped down off the rock. "Ready to grill some brats?"

"I am getting kind of hungry," she said, taking his hand. The two made their way back down to the cabin. Once there, Wil opened the refrigerator and grabbed some brats. "I'll fire up the grill if you want to grab what you want to go with the brats. I should have asked—are brats okay?"

"I'd love to have them."

Wil was cooking the brats when Kelsey joined him with potato salad, ketchup, and mustard. She also brought out a couple of beers. She set everything up on a small picnic table that was sitting alongside the cabin facing the open area that included Box Elder Creek. She stood by him and watched him grill the brats. "I've never seen a person grill anything until I arrived in South Dakota."

Wil turned the brats over once more. "Well, you're going to have to prepare what you want on your brats because they're done."

She laughed. "I think I can handle it."

The two sat at the table and ate their supper in silence. Kelsey pointed. "Is that a bear?"

Wil peered over where she was pointing. "It sure is."

"Will it come to the cabin?"

"No, it will drink its fill of water out of Box Elder Creek and make its way into the Hills behind the cabin."

"Wow, so cool. Do you see them often?"

"I see pretty much everything out here. At times I hear animals rustling outside the cabin. I'm not sure if it's a mountain lion or some other kind of critter, although I did see mountain lion tracks in the back one morning." Wil had kept his eyes on the bear. "There he goes."

They both watched as the bear stared over at them and the cabin, then darted into the hills behind the cabin. The sun started to set as they were finishing up their meal. Kelsey jumped up and started to clean things while Wil made sure the fire was completely out. She carried everything inside and Wil followed.

"I should probably take you back to Deadwood."

She peered into his eyes and was about to say something but stopped.

"What?" Wil shrugged.

Kelsey's eyes twinkled. "Nothing. I'm ready to go back to the hotel."

Chapter 4

Kelsey and the rest of her friends drove up to Blue Bell Lodge on Wednesday morning for horseback riding. She was quiet on the ride up into the Black Hills.

"Kelsey, is everything okay?" Clinton asked.

She glanced at him. "Yes, I'm just thinking about things."

Lisa grinned. "I bet you're thinking about that handsome guide we had. Wil Bolton."

Kelsey looked around. "No, I'm thinking about how beautiful it is around here."

Alexis joined in. "I'd sure be thinking about that handsome guy. He's probably six-one with those gorgeous blue eyes, and I love his long hair with the bandana. By the way, where did you go yesterday?"

She peered at Alexis. "I went to Rapid City to do some shopping for clothes, had a taco, and spent the afternoon in the bookstore."

"How boring of a life do you have," JJ commented.

Kelsey grinned. "Pretty boring."

Clinton frowned. "Is that why you got in after dark?"

"Are you spying on Kelsey?" Alexis asked.

"No, I just saw her walking into the hotel around ten."

Kelsey sighed. "I went out for a walk around Deadwood."

"If you say so," Clinton said.

Kelsey glared at him. "It's really none of your business what I do on my vacation."

They arrived at Blue Bell Lodge fifteen minutes later. After they were saddled with their horses, they rode into the Black Hills. The guide stopped them about halfway through the trip so they could enjoy the view.

Kelsey, who was riding right ahead of Alexis, turned to her voice.

"That must be the Badlands. It looks so much different than the Midwest."

"Think you're right. I'm excited about going there."

"Maybe we should call the forest service and see if we can hire Wil Bolton to guide us through the Badlands."

Kelsey didn't respond.

Alexis continued. "I think I will. He's awfully cute, and I wouldn't mind spending a night with him before I left."

"What about JJ?"

"What about him? I'll never see Wil Bolton again after we leave here."

"Wow, I can't believe you."

Alexis laughed. "Don't tell me you haven't thought

about hooking up with Wil Bolton?"

Again, Kelsey didn't respond.

"That's where you were yesterday? You spent time with him. Did you get him into bed with you?"

"I didn't, Alexis. How crude can you be? I just don't jump into bed with any guy I meet."

"That's the difference between you and me. He's handsome, and I like handsome guys. Did you tell him you were rich?"

Kelsey glared at her. "I didn't, and don't you dare say anything about us having money."

"Aha, you do like him. You're no different than I am. Your fiancé, Nolan Gant, is waiting for you back in Chicago, and you're thinking about a South Dakota country boy."

"We'll never see Wil again."

They continued their horseback ride back to Blue Bell Lodge where they stopped in for lunch.

"Look at this, buffalo burgers. I wonder what they taste like," JJ said.

"I'm going to try one," Clinton said.

All of them ordered buffalo burger meals with a beer. Once they were finished, they hiked around the lodge trails for the next couple of hours.

"Wow, this is so amazing," Kelsey said as they stopped at a group of rocks overlooking a valley. "Are those deer going through down there?"

"They sure are," Clinton said. He pulled out his cell phone and took some photos. "They'll never believe us that we saw a bunch of deer in person."

"Why wouldn't they?" Lisa asked. "There are deer back in Chicago. Are you that dumb?"

Clinton glared at her. "Why are you always so

cruel?”

“Cruel? Think about what you just said. There are deer everywhere.”

“What about a mountain lion?” Kelsey asked, pointing away from them.

They all turned and looked at the lion who was staring at them from a distance. Clinton started taking photos of it. Just like that the mountain lion raced toward them, and they started running away. They heard a shot, and the mountain lion hit the ground.

“What the hell just happened?” Alexis asked.

“Somebody shot it,” JJ said.

They turned at Wil’s voice. “You never run from a mountain lion or any wild animal for that matter.”

“Did you kill it?” Clinton asked.

“No, I tranquilized it. We had word there was a mountain lion seen up here, and I was sent to find it. I found it.” He gazed at Kelsey and turned to the others. “Are you okay?”

Kelsey nodded. “A little scared, but we’ll be okay. Thanks for showing up when you did.”

“You’re welcome. I’ll have to call it in, so you can head back on your trail.”

They stayed where they were as Wil called the forest service. “Amanda, I found the mountain lion and it’s sleeping.”

“You okay?”

“Yes, but it put a scare in some of our tourists from Chicago.”

“Are they okay?”

“They seem to be.”

“They’re on their way to pick up the mountain lion.”

Once he got off the phone, Kelsey asked him what would happen to the big cat.

"They'll transport him back to his habitat."

"How do they know where he belongs?" Clinton asked.

Wil bent down and grabbed an ear tag. "Tagging studies the long-range movements of animals and determines their life span. Tags also teach us about the area the animal occupies, its movement throughout the area, and its daily activities in its habitat."

"Does it say where?" JJ asked.

"It looks like somewhere in Montana."

"How did it get this far?" JJ asked.

Wil peered up at him. "Most wild animals travel long distances in a short period of time. Changing the subject, how was your horseback riding?"

"How did you know we went horseback riding?" Alexis asked.

"You're in the Blue Bell Lodge area, which is mostly known for horseback riding. People love the scenery."

"The view is gorgeous," Kelsey said. "We could see the Badlands from on top of one of those hills."

"Yes, you can."

Alexis chimed in. "We're thinking about going to the Badlands tomorrow. Can you guide us there?"

"That's up to my boss."

They all turned when a vehicle made its way up the road. It stopped, and a couple of forest-service people jumped out. Wil helped them load the mountain lion. Once the cat was loaded, they took off and Wil turned to the group.

"I'll hike back with you to the lodge."

"Where's your vehicle?" Kelsey asked as they walked back.

"At Blue Bell Lodge. I've been checking the trails for the mountain lion for the past couple of hours."

"Is it normal to chase an animal for that long?"

"I did it for a couple of days one time."

"Wow. How do you do it?"

"I love the outdoors."

When they arrived back at Blue Bell Lodge thirty minutes later, Wil climbed into his pickup, and started to leave when Kelsey walked up to his truck. He rolled down his window and said, "They're having a quarterly social gathering tonight. It's short notice, but I wondered if you would join me."

"Be your date?"

He nodded.

"I'm sorry but I can't."

Chapter 5

That evening Wil arrived at the social dressed in a nice sports coat. He had cut his hair and trimmed his beard. Wil looked around and saw Kelsey talking to a guy. She obviously had a boyfriend which was why he figured she couldn't join him. She wore a green party dress, and he appreciated she didn't go overboard with the makeup. He preferred her natural look. A few minutes later, he turned to a soft touch on his arm. "Wow, you look gorgeous."

Kelsey's face flushed. "Thank you. I'd say you look nice also. And you cut your hair. What's up with that?"

"Formal event, so I figured I should. When you said you didn't want to come with me, I figured out it was because you have a boyfriend."

"About that. I do have a fiancé in Chicago."

She was getting ready to say something else when Hampton and his wife walked over. "Wil, glad you could make it. And who do we have here?"

"This is Kelsey Lawrence visiting from Chicago."

"Nice to meet you, Ms. Lawrence," he said.

"And you too," Kelsey smiled, turning to his wife. "And you also, ma'am."

After a few minutes of chit-chat, the man turned to leave "Enjoy yourselves," he said, taking his wife's hand.

"They seem to be a nice couple," Kelsey said after they left.

"He's been a good boss, and his wife is an angel. She's always been good to the employees at the forest service by bringing baked goods and remembering birthdays, weddings, and other special moments."

"That's sweet."

"Should we grab some food and mingle?"

Kelsey nodded. They took their place in a line for the buffet. Wil and Kelsey approached two couples who were sitting at a table.

"Can we join you?" Wil asked.

The older gentleman nodded. "Aren't you Wil Bolton with the forest service?"

"I am, sir. And you are?"

"We have a cattle ranch just north of the forest service on the road to Belle Fourche a couple of miles away. They said you were good at tracking animals."

"I'm sent out to follow prints, and that's about it. Nothing more."

"I'm sorry to hear that because I was hoping you'd take us elk hunting in northern California."

"I'm sorry I've never been to California and wouldn't have the faintest idea of where the best hunting spots were."

"I understand that you haven't been there, but I

also know from talking to people you have a knack for finding what you're looking for. Take for example the three young people who were hiking near Crows Nest Peak last week."

"They had lights, so it was easy to find."

"Yes, but you brought them down after dark in a treacherous area of the Black Hills."

"I know the lay of the land."

The older lady joined in. "You sure are a modest fellow."

The younger gentleman leaned forward. "We have land just outside of the Black Hills National Forest outside of Spearfish and are starting to see signs of mountain lion tracks. Are they becoming more prevalent in the Black Hills?"

Wil finished chewing a bit of his pork sandwich. "They are moving this way from the Rockies, but I can't tell you why. Some believe it is because of the encroachment of humans in their habitat, but that's just a theory. No one knows for sure what's causing the increase in the animals."

The older man gazed over at Kelsey. "Are you this young man's wife?"

"No sir, he's a friend. I'm actually from Chicago and just visiting."

His wife eyed Kelsey. "You two will live a long and prosperous life together."

Kelsey blushed. "Well, I don't know about that. I'm engaged to a guy in Chicago. We're getting married in August."

The group suddenly grew quiet and concentrated on their meal. Then Hampton stepped up to the mic to talk about the forest service. He provided a twenty-minute presentation and took questions. One dealt with the increase in mountain lion tracks.

"I'll have Wil Bolton provide some insight on that. Wil, would you please join me?"

When Wil took a deep breath, Kelsey whispered to him. "You'll be just fine. Go on."

Wil slowly stepped up to the stage, turning to Hampton. "Thanks for putting me on the spot, boss," he said. Hampton slapped him on the back as the crowd laughed. He turned to the crowd and blew out a breath. "You're right, bears, mountain lions, and bighorn sheep are in the forest. In the past they were rarely seen. Now we're seeing animal tracks more and more. Just this afternoon I tranquilized a mountain lion who was ready to pounce on a group of hikers."

Gasps filled the air.

Wil took a moment to take a sip of water. "A month ago, a man woke up and opened his cabin door. A mountain lion was fast asleep on his porch. As you can imagine, both he and the mountain lion had quite a scare. I had to tranquilize two mountain lions a few months ago. Before that, I'd done one but never two at a time. What is happening has a lot to do with the encroachment of people living in the Black Hills. The animals have nowhere to go, so animals and people have to figure out a way to live together. It does make it difficult for people like me. Visitors fail to heed the warning signs, and the animals are looking for a new habitat."

He surveyed the crowd of diners. "All I can say is let us know as soon as possible when you find tracks, and by no means hunt the animals by yourself because when cornered they are very dangerous." After answering a few questions, Wil stepped down and joined Kelsey.

She grabbed his hand. "Good job."

"Thanks."

The older man joined in. "You have what it takes to go a long way, son."

Wil's eyes widened. "What are you trying to say, sir?"

"You said it when you were up there that animals and humans are trying to figure a way to coexist in today's world, and it's going to take people who think outside the box to come up with solutions."

"Mr. Hampton does a wonderful job."

"I realize that, and I'm not criticizing the man because this forest service does a wonderful job. All I'm saying is that you think quick on your feet, and that's what is needed in critical situations. Just think about it."

"Thank you, sir. You've given me something to think about."

The group talked for a bit longer around the table before a band started playing.

He touched her hand. "Would you like to dance, Kelsey?"

"I'd love to." Kelsey put her arms around Wil's neck. "I had so much fun tonight. This is a perfect ending to our evening."

Both were silent as they danced. When they started to say something at the same time, they both giggled. "Go ahead," Wil said.

Kelsey smiled. "I was just wondering how you're able to handle all of the different aspects of working for the forest service. You guide people, you track down animals, and finally get up and speak about things happening in the wildlife service."

"I don't know what to say."

"What were you going to say?"

"Nothing really."

She peered into his eyes. "What was it?" When he didn't say anything, Kelsey prompted him. "You can tell me anything, and it's okay."

Wil took a deep breath. "I had thought about asking you to spend the night with me, but that wouldn't be right because you're engaged. I'm sorry."

She peered into his eyes. "You're right. I can't because I'm engaged."

Chapter 6

When Wil walked into the office around ten the next morning, Amanda just pointed to the boss's office. He shrugged. "Again?"

She grinned.

Wil made his way into Hampton's office and stuck his head in. "You asked for me?"

"Yes, for some reason this group from Chicago believes you're the best and want you to take them on a tour of the Badlands. They're waiting for you at Cadillac Jacks in Deadwood, and it's an overnighter. They've already arranged cabins for everyone to stay in."

When Wil didn't say anything, Hampton laughed. "Enjoy yourself. Good things may come out of this."

Not sure what Hampton meant, he threw some gear into the back of the forest-service van that held ten passengers, then drove fifty-six miles from Custer to Deadwood on Highway 385 arriving at Cadillac Jacks around eleven-thirty. The group was waiting in front of the casino when he pulled up. He noticed there was an additional person.

"Good to see you again, Wil," Alexis said. "We added another guy to the group. Meet Nolan Gant, Kelsey's fiancé."

Wil had a quick peek at Kelsey who spun away. Nolan Gant came over and proffered his hand. "Great to meet you, Mr. Bolton. Kelsey has told me you've been very accommodating for the group, and I am looking forward to the trip to the Badlands."

"Let's load your gear into the back of the van, and we'll head to Wall Drug for lunch and some souvenir shopping, then we'll continue to the Badlands." Wil opened the back of the van, and the group handed him their luggage.

Kelsey was the last one to give him her bag. She gently touched his hand. "This is awfully awkward. I'm sorry I didn't know he would be joining us."

"No worries. You told me you were engaged."

Kelsey eyed Wil. "Can we talk?"

"We should be going."

The group arrived at Wall Drug just after one. Wil found a place to park and turned to the group. "We'll leave here at three, which gives you a couple of hours to eat and chase down some souvenirs. The t-shirts, jade, and Black Hills gold jewelry are especially popular here."

Lisa hurried over to Wil. "How about you join me for lunch?"

Wil took a deep breath and glanced over at Kelsey. "I should probably stick to myself because I'm here to guide you."

Her lower lip protruded in a pout. "You had no

problems spending time with Kelsey," she said, hurrying away.

Wil shook his head and went through the line for food after the others had gathered their food and found a table in the corner. Kelsey scooted over so Wil could sit down next to her.

"This food really tastes good," Nolan said, after taking his first bite of his cheeseburger. "Good idea, Bolton."

Wil just nodded.

"I'm sure Kelsey told you we're engaged to be married in a couple of months."

"She mentioned it," Wil said. "I'm happy for you. You've hit the jackpot."

Nolan grinned. "I have. It's a match made in heaven."

Kelsey took a deep breath. "That's enough, Nolan. I'm sure Wil doesn't want to hear about our marriage plans."

Alexis jumped in. "August thirtieth will be here before you know it. Do you have the venue and everything set up, Kelsey?"

"Still working on it," Kelsey said.

Nolan looked at her. "I thought everything was set for the Stan Mansion in Chicago."

JJ grinned. "That's got to cost a lot of money."

"It does," Kelsey said softly.

~

Kelsey was wandering around Wall Drug purchasing jade and Black Hills Gold jewelry while the others were dawdling around different areas of the huge store. She was not paying attention and then screamed when a T-Rex breathed fire toward her. She fell backwards and peered up into Wil's eyes as he caught her. "Oh my, that scared the crap out of me," Kelsey said. "Why didn't you tell me?" She smacked Wil lightly on the arm.

"I didn't know."

She couldn't pull her eyes away until he finally let her go. "Thank you for catching me. I'm sorry about all of this."

"It's normal to be frightened by something you're not used to."

She took a deep breath. "That isn't what I meant, and you know it."

He gently took her shoulders. "Listen to me, there is nothing you have to explain to me. You're engaged to marry a guy who has a lot of money, and I don't blame you."

"It's not like that."

Wil put up his hand. "You had better finish shopping because we're leaving in fifteen minutes."

Kelsey watched as Wil walked away from her. She wiped away a tear wishing she could explain, but he wouldn't listen to her. He was right; she shouldn't care because she was engaged, but in her heart, she felt she had blown any type of relationship with Wil.

Familiar arms circled her from behind. "This is where you went," Nolan said. "Did you find everything you were looking for?"

"I did. How about you?"

"I bought you a nice necklace. Here, let me put it around your neck."

Once he snapped it on, she looked at a small cross. "It's really pretty," she said.

He grabbed her hand and the two headed out of

Wall Drug toward the van. Wil was sitting on a bench talking to Lisa when the two walked up. Kelsey noticed Lisa had moved closer to Wil when she saw her.

"Kelsey, Nolan, did you find everything you were looking for?" she asked.

Nolan pointed toward the necklace. "What do you think? Isn't it beautiful?"

"Wow. True love," Lisa said. "Don't you think so, Wil?"

Wil eyed Kelsey and turned to Lisa. "We should probably head to our next destination."

Chapter 7

Wil pulled the van into a prairie dog village, and everyone climbed out.

"What's this?" Kelsey asked.

"People can feed prairie dogs here," Wil said.

"With what?" she asked.

Wil turned and pointed to the shed. They walked in and purchased some peanuts to feed the prairie dogs. Every time Kelsey walked up to them, they scrambled away.

Wil slowly inched close to one. He laid the peanut down and the prairie dog grabbed it with his two front paws, keeping his eyes on Wil as he ate.

Kelsey took some photos with her cell phone. It was another half hour before Kelsey was finally able to coax a prairie dog near her. Wil shot some photos.

After a half hour, Wil started the drive through Badlands National Park, stopping at the Badlands Wall. Nolan grabbed Kelsey's hand and the two walked to the lookout area.

"This is so beautiful," Kelsey said.

"I'm glad you like it," Nolan said, wrapping his arms around her.

Kelsey's eyes popped over to Wil who stared at the Badlands. She gently pushed back. "It's kind of warm."

"I read it does heat up in the Badlands. I hope we have air conditioning in our cabin."

They spent another thirty minutes viewing the Big Badlands Overlook. A marker explained to the tourists that they could view the eastern portion of the Badlands wall and erosional features extending from Kadoka to Wall.

Wil joined them and pointed out an area in the southeastern horizon. "Since it's a clear day, you can see Eagle Nest Butte which is situated next to the town of Wanblee."

"That is so cool," Lisa said.

Wil explained that the geologic deposits contained one of the world's richest fossil beds. "Ancient horses and rhinoceros once roamed here. The park consists of more than 240,000 acres. Badlands is a mixed-grass prairie that consists of bighorn sheep, prairie dogs, and black-footed ferrets."

Kelsey peered up at Wil. "How old are the Badlands?"

"Millions of years old. Can't be certain. The Badland formations erode about an inch a year."
He pointed at the different formations. "See the different rock types? The formations contain sandstone, siltstone, mudstone, claystone, limestone, volcanic ash, and shale."

Once they were finished taking pictures, Lisa turned to him. "There seem to be different colors among the rocks."

"Correct. The layers correspond with different eras over the years. For instance, the Pierre Shale forms the bottom layer and it was deposited somewhere between sixty-nine and seventy-five million years ago. A shallow inland sea known as the Western Interior Seaway provided the deposits." He continued. "There are four other layers on top. The youngest geologic formation is the Sharps Formation which formed close to thirty million years ago. The base of this formation is the Rockford Ash. It came from ash from eruptions in the Great Basin where Utah and Nevada are located today."

Lisa placed her arm into Wil's. "You're a wealth of knowledge."

Wil pulled away. "It's what I enjoy."

The group spent the afternoon hiking the trails around the Badlands and taking photos. Later they pulled into the restaurant in the Badlands where they had rented a cabin for the night.

"What are you going to have?" Clinton asked.

Wil thought about it. "I understand the Indian taco is really good. I think I'll have that."

"I'll order that also."

Many ordered the Indian taco while others ordered hamburgers and salads. The sun had vanished by the time they were finishing up.

"I have something you need to see," Wil said, walking up the trail.

"Where are we going?" Alexis asked.

"Up into the rocks to look into the sky and see how beautiful it is at night."

The two joined the others who already had the

same idea. They found an isolated area and climbed on a rock. Alexis snuggled close to JJ. "This is so beautiful. I could stay here all night."

He held her tightly and pointed up at the sky. "You never see this in a big city."

"No we don't."

The two were quiet for another ten minutes before Wil pointed at a shooting star. Kelsey jumped up. "I've never seen a shooting star in Chicago, or Illinois for that matter."

"There are just so many other lights that hide the beauty."

Nolan pulled Kelsey toward him and kissed her gently. "I love this, and I'm glad I'm seeing it with you."

Kelsey peered at Wil who was staring up at the night sky. She glanced back at Nolan. "It is beautiful out here."

The group spent a couple more hours enjoying the vista. At times they would talk quietly, but most of the time they silently enjoyed the beauty. It was past midnight when Wil stood up, and they headed back to the cabins, a fifteen-minute stroll along a trail in the darkness.

After everyone went into their cabins, Wil sat out on a picnic table staring into the sky. Kelsey joined him. "The first time we ever met you were staring at cobblestones, but now you're staring into the sky."

Wil turned to her. "You're not tired?"

"No, I'm having too much fun enjoying the night."

"I know what you mean, but I figured you and Nolan had some catching up to do."

She frowned. "It's safe to say I'm not really in the

mood tonight. I want to enjoy the beauty as much as I can."

"If I were Nolan, I'd be pretty disappointed."

"Why?" she asked.

"You're a unique gal and one I'm sure Nolan wants to spend as much time with as he can."

She blushed. "There'll be plenty of time for that after we're married. That is, if we do get married."

Wil immediately stood up. "I'll escort you back to your cabin. Tomorrow will be another busy day."

She joined him. "I appreciate you walking me back to the cabin even though it's within walking distance."

"Anything can happen in the Black Hills."

The next morning they took the Badlands Loop back toward Rapid City. Wil made two stops allowing the group to walk trails and take photos of the Badlands. They stopped at the Rapid City Mall so the group could do some last-minute shopping before heading back to Chicago the next day.

Wil was sitting at a table drinking a soda when Kelsey came over and sat down with him.

"Did you buy anything special?"

Her cheeks warmed. "A particular item for an exceptional guy."

Wil grinned. "Nolan is one lucky guy."

"Why would you say that?"

"In another couple of months, he'll be marrying the most beautiful gal that anyone has ever seen."

Kelsey lowered her eyes. "Thank you."

"Are you ready to go back to Chicago?"

Kelsey searched the food court. "I've been thinking about staying here a bit longer."

"Why?"

She peered into his eyes. "I just have some unfinished business I want to take care of."

"What type of unfinished business could you have in South Dakota?"

"I'll tell you someday."

They both turned to a young man's voice. "Wow, what a nice figure. How would you like to crawl in bed with me?"

Wil stood and faced the guy who was with two others. "Walk away."

"Are you her brother, or are you sleeping with her?"

Will took a deep breath. "I said, walk away." He drew the words out. The three guys were about to say something when a police officer walked over. They disappeared quickly.

"Problems here?"

"We're good," Wil said.

The officer stared at Kelsey and turned back to Wil. "Several gang members hang out at the mall. They like to hit on girls, so watch yourself."

"Will do, sir. Thanks."

After he left, Kelsey stared at Wil. "You weren't afraid of them. Just like you weren't afraid of the mountain lions. Are you some sort of highly trained killer?"

Wil almost choked on his drink. "No, I'm not. I just don't spook easily."

"I see that."

They chatted some more when the others joined them. Wil counted the people there. "All here." He stood up. "I'll take you back to Deadwood."

They were heading through the parking lot to the

pickup when the three young men sauntered up to them. The guy who had spoken before leered at Kelsey. "I've been waiting for you."

Nolan took a step forward. "Back off, punk," he said.

The boy pulled out a knife and waved it at Nolan. "If you want to be gutted, keep talking."

Nolan backed off, and Kelsey squeezed behind Wil. Once Nolan wasn't a threat, the boy turned back toward Kelsey and Wil. "Get out of the way. I'll take this one."

Wil didn't say anything but continued to stare at the thug.

"Did you hear me, or are you deaf?" The guy lunged for her.

Wil grabbed Kelsey's hand and pulled her away.

"I said get out of my way."

Wil whipped around, grabbed the guy's wrist, and snapped it behind him.

"You broke my arm."

Wil whispered, "Leave her alone, or I'll break more than just your arm." He let the guy go, took Kelsey's hand, and started walking. When she started to say something, Wil glared at her. "Don't say one word."

Chapter 8

They arrived back in Deadwood around three-thirty when Wil dropped them off at Cadillac Jacks. Once the gear was unloaded, Wil was climbing back into the van to drive back to Custer when Kelsey handed him a card.

"Please join us tonight?"

Before Wil could say anything, she hurried away into Cadillac Jacks. Wil drove toward Custer arriving around five. He took care of the van, hopped into his truck, and opened the card. It was an invitation to a social gathering at the Lodge at Deadwood at seven, and it was a dress-up occasion.

Wil took a deep breath, threw it on the seat, and drove toward Nemo. An hour later he pulled up to his cabin. Just as he walked in, his cell phone rang. It was one of his friends, Laney Pruitt. "Laney, what's going on? Is everything okay?"

"Yes, it is. I was wondering if you were going to that social event tonight at the Lodge at Deadwood."

"I hadn't planned on it. Why?"

"Bailey and I were invited, and I thought it would be fun. Bailey is out of town for the weekend so was wondering if you would join me."

Wil didn't hesitate. "I could never turn you down."

She laughed. "Great, can you pick me up?"

"I'll pick you up at six-thirty or so."

"I'll be waiting."

A few hours later, Wil knocked on the door of Laney and Bailey's house across from the Lead-Deadwood High School track and field complex. When Laney opened the door, Wil looked up stunned. "Wow, I've never seen you so beautiful."

She blushed. "Wil, stop it. I just threw on a nice dress and did some stuff to my hair and my face. I will say you look much better than I've ever seen you. Are you thinking about meeting a gal tonight?"

He laughed. "Not really."

The two arrived just after seven and walked into the Lodge at Deadwood that sat on top of a hill just outside the city. The Lodge at Deadwood was one of the newer gambling facilities in Deadwood.

Laney placed her arm into Wil's. "This is really nice." A gal walked over with a tray of drinks. The two grabbed glasses of wine. "High class," Laney said.

She sipped her glass of wine then peered up at Wil preparing to say something when she turned to look where he was staring and saw a beautiful light brown-haired gal, her arm linked with a handsome guy with blond hair. "Is that the gal you're interested in?"

"What?" Wil asked, turning his attention to her.

"That gal over there. You've been looking at her quite intently."

"She's with her fiancé."

"Oh, I see," Laney said quietly. "Don't worry. I'll protect you until you make a move on her, and then I'll bow out."

Wil glared at her. "It won't happen, and you know that."

She reached up and kissed him on the cheek. "For someone who is a daredevil out in the forest, you sure are shy when it comes to dealing with gals."

"Wild animals are much easier. And don't ask me why because I don't know."

Laney laughed. "Okay, I won't. Well, enjoy yourself. Guess what, she's coming your way."

Wil rolled his eyes. "You're relishing this, aren't you?"

She smirked. "It's kind of cool seeing Wil Bolton squirm."

Kelsey and Nolan joined them. "Wil Bolton, it's wonderful to see you again," Nolan said. "What do you think of this party we're putting on?"

"It's nice."

"And who do we have here?" he asked.

Laney spoke up. "Laney Pruitt, I'm Wil's date for this evening and hopefully into the future. And you are?" she said, looking directly at Kelsey.

"Kelsey Lawrence."

"And you know Wil how?"

Kelsey peered up at Wil. "He's led us on a couple of trails in the Black Hills and Badlands over the past couple of days."

Nolan jumped in. "We're engaged to be married in August. We just wanted to throw this party to thank everyone who was part of our experience throughout the week."

Wil noticed Kelsey rolling her eyes when he made the last comment.

"How long have you two known each other?" Kelsey asked.

"For two years," Laney said. "I thought he may have told you about us."

Kelsey frowned. "He didn't say anything, but then again Nolan and I are together."

"Oh," was all Laney said. She turned to Wil. "I came to dance." She took his hand, and the two went out onto the dance floor.

"What was that all about?" Wil asked.

"She's really into you, best friend."

"How would you know that?"

"Simple, she hasn't taken her eyes off of you since she first saw you come in, and she winced when I kissed you on the cheek. Not only that, she was clearly shocked and hurt when I told her we've known each other for two years."

"Enough. You'll always be my best friend, but I'm not going to do anything to any gal who has her whole life ahead of her with a rich guy."

"And why can't she have a life with you?"

"Get real. I have nothing."

She grinned. "Has she seen your lovely cabin?"

"She has."

"And she didn't run away?"

"Of course not." Wil glared at her.

"That's a start. I've only seen you look at her for a few seconds, but I already know you care more about her than you ever did Lydia, and you two were pretty close. And unless I miss my guess, she has the same feelings for you."

"It won't happen. End of story."

"Okay, Wil, if you say so," she said, laying her head against his shoulder.

~

Kelsey sat on the side of the bed slipping off her heels. She stared over at Nolan who was just walking through the door.

"A wonderful night," he said. "We made some solid connections tonight."

Kelsey let out a breath. "Why are you even here? We both know that our relationship is over and really never should have started."

He sat near her. "That's your opinion, but your father has a different expectation. He believes we should be together."

"Then he should marry you because I'm not walking down the aisle with you in August. I've decided I'd rather stay single than marry any guy who dotes on my father. You realize that he is a manipulator and at times an evil man."

"Because he's a billionaire? How do you think you were able to get your start?"

Kelsey glared at him. "I made my money because I have good employees who know what they're doing and nothing more."

"Why did you agree to marry me when I asked you?"

"I'm still trying to figure that out because I really have never loved you. Our family requires us to marry people who have money, so that may be part of it."

He grinned at her. "And I'm sure what happens in bed was part of it?"

"Don't flatter yourself."

She stood up, grabbed her heels, and finished packing her suitcase.

"Where are you going?"

"To find another room. We're through."

He grabbed her arm. "Is it because of Wil Bolton?"

"He's none of your concern."

Nolan released her arm. "You fell for a country bum. How tragic is that for a rich gal. Your father won't be too happy."

"Oh, I'm so tired of my father and others dictating how I run my life. I'll decide who I fall in love with and who I choose to be with for the rest of my life. And you're right, I care about Wil, but I'm not sure if he's even thought about me a second, but I'll find out over the next week. Go back to my father and tell him exactly what I'm doing because I don't care."

~

Wil was sitting on his porch Sunday afternoon when a rental car drove up to his carport. Kelsey stepped out. "I thought you were heading back to Chicago?"

She grinned at him. "I have some unfinished business here in South Dakota, so I decided to stay another week."

"What about work? What about Nolan?"

"What are you drinking?"

"I'm sorry, I should have asked if you wanted some coffee. I'll be right back. Sugar and cream?"

"One teaspoon of each, please," she said.

He came out with a cup of coffee for Kelsey. She sipped some of it and held it with both hands. "This is good."

"Thanks. Now why are you here?"

"Yeah, about that. I need to tell you some things. First, it is true I do work in the clothing industry, but I also own a multi-million-dollar clothing and design business, and my father, Hank Lawrence, is a multi-billionaire. As you can tell, I come from a rich family."

"Wow," Wil said. "I was kissed by a billionaire's daughter. That was a first."

She glared at him. "Are you going to be a jerk about this whole thing?"

He didn't back down. "A jerk? You lied to me. Why couldn't you tell me who you really were?"

She sighed. "One reason—when guys find out who I really am, they're never themselves, and I wanted to find out who you really were, not someone who bows to my wishes or tries to impress me. From the first moment I saw you I felt differently about you than I have any other guy." Kelsey took a sip of her coffee. "The second reason I'm here is because I'm trying to figure out if I want to take a chance with a guy who's completely different than what I'm used to."

"Wow, did you just say that you were trying to figure out if I was good enough to hang out with a rich girl? Why would you even think that? After all, you're engaged."

"That does sound patronizing, doesn't it? But please understand in my world I could lose everything that I've worked for, and I'm not sure if I want to do that. I wanted someone who I could be myself around, and I found it in you." When he didn't respond, Kelsey continued. "Remember when you asked me to spend the night with you, and I said, 'I can't. I'm engaged.'"

He nodded.

"I should have never said that because I truly wanted to spend the night with you, and I still do."

Wil looked at her. "It'll never happen."

"Is it because of Laney?"

"No, Laney is my best friend, and she's engaged to marry Bailey Blue."

"The guy who flies helicopters?"

Wil nodded.

Kelsey laughed. "Perfect. You call me a liar, and you did the same damn thing. Why would you do that?"

He took her in his arms and kissed her passionately on the lips. "That's why. I'm in love with you, but I realize I have no chance because you're rich and you're marrying a rich guy. Why would you want to be with me?"

She took his hands. "You should have never done that. Now you'll never get rid of me. That kiss shot through my heart, and it was what I was hoping to feel. One thing you need to know about me: I don't care about money; I just care about a guy who steals my heart, and you just did it with that kiss. As for Nolan, I broke off our engagement on Friday night. I'm staying here for another week because you're my unfinished business. It's up to you whether I stay longer." She spun around and headed to her car.

"Where are you going?"

She eyed him. "I'm staying at Cadillac Jacks for the week."

He sighed. "I have an extra bedroom, and you can stay here."

She stared at him. "Are you sure? Because I can tell you right now, I'll never stay all week in that bedroom."

Wil grinned. "How about if we take it slow? Let's start with a dinner tonight at my former girlfriend's house?"

Kelsey laughed. "It's a date." She walked over to her car.

"Where are you going?" Wil asked.

She grinned. "Your friend, Laney, may have told me you two weren't an item, so I brought my clothes with me hoping you'd ask me to stay."

Chapter 9

Wil and Kelsey drove over to Lead to a supper that Bailey and Laney were throwing for friends of theirs. The two, who had been dating each other since college, would be marrying in two weeks.

"How did Nolan handle the news you were breaking off your engagement?" Wil asked Kelsey as they drove toward Lead.

"It's been brewing ever since I met him. I don't know why I ever said I'd marry him. The only thing I can think of is he has money, and that is what is expected of a Lawrence, but that isn't what I want. What I said earlier is true. You stole my heart, and that's what I always wanted. If truth be known, you did it the first time I met you counting those cobblestone bricks."

"I felt the same way when I looked up at you in that green miniskirt. I had never seen a gal as pretty as you."

"Where do we go from here?"

"Simple, we take it slowly and see how it goes. What about your business?"

"Yeah, I'll have to think about that. It'll all depend on how my week turns out. You and I fall in love, then I don't have a problem selling the business."

"You lied to me once more."

"What?" Her eyes went wide.

"You said you weren't a gambler, but here you are possibly selling your business because you love a guy."

She grinned. "Isn't love grand?"

The two arrived at the house in Lead. Wil had purchased a cherry pie that they brought with them to the supper engagement.

When he knocked on the door, Bailey answered. "Wil, good to see you. And who do we have here?"

Laney, who had walked up behind Bailey, spoke for Kelsey. "Wil's new girlfriend? Meet Kelsey Lawrence."

Before anyone could answer, Laney grabbed Kelsey's hand and dragged her into the house. Bailey grinned at Wil. "Good for you. She's a beauty."

"It isn't what you think."

"Then what is it?"

Wil frowned. "I'm really not sure. I care about her, but it's moving too quick. She said she loves me, but who knows?"

Bailey put his arm around Wil. "Good, buddy, a gal that beautiful doesn't say that if she doesn't mean it."

"Maybe. We're just going to take it slow."

"Where's she staying?"

"In my cabin."

Bailey laughed. "If she's staying in your cabin, she

must be in love with you."

"And what is that supposed to mean?"

"Your cabin will fall over at the first strong windstorm."

Wil and Bailey walked into the living room where Kelsey was talking to Laney and Amanda. She peered up at him and waved her pinkie finger at him. He waved back.

"Wil Bolton, how have you been?"

Wil turned to a familiar voice. "What are you doing here?"

"You didn't forget me. That's good news. I'm looking for something, and I want you to help me."

Wil shook his head. "Last time I helped you, we almost got hauled in for distributing drugs across the Mexican border."

"I'm out of that business now. What I'm looking for is a special artifact in the Black Hills."

"What would that be?"

He looked around and then whispered. "Possible prehistoric dinosaur skeleton."

"Yeah, right."

"Several have been found in South Dakota including the counties of Fall River, Custer, and Harding, among others. It's out there, and you know every inch of the Black Hills National Forest. My benefactor can pay you handsomely. If I remember right, you've always wanted to travel the world and look for treasures. You can start right here in South Dakota."

"I don't know. I still remember the last time you and I worked together."

"That was three years ago, and I've changed. I

haven't messed with drugs since that incident. At least let me set something up for you to talk with the benefactor?"

Wil hesitated. "Okay, I can do that."

"Good. He'll contact you this week. You won't regret this."

After he left, Wil shook his head and mumbled, "I bet you I will."

"Do you talk to yourself often? Is that something I should be aware of?"

Wil turned to Kelsey. "No, not really. I just met a guy I haven't seen in a couple of years, and he wants me to find something for him."

"You're good at that sort of thing."

"Yeah, but the last time we did business together, it involved transporting drugs from Mexico."

"Oh. And you're going to work with him?"

"I told him I'd talk to his benefactor. He's looking for a dinosaur fossil."

"That's legitimate. There are many dinosaur fossil digs around the world and right here in South Dakota."

Wil eyed her. "Knowledgeable gal, aren't you?"

She beamed. "My father is into finding artifacts and treasures around the world. He's trying to finagle his way into a partnership with Dr. Isaac Regret, an anthropologist at the University of Illinois in Champaign. Dr. Regret is working with something called Treasure Paradise. You really should talk to the professor because you two would be a good fit."

"I'll think about it."

She handed him some chicken wings. "These are very good."

Wil tasted the one she gave him. "It is good. Tastes

like honey barbecue or something like that.”

"There are plenty of them here.”

Wil and Kelsey spent a couple of hours at the party, and it was around nine when they headed back to Nemo. They arrived around nine-thirty.

"Would you like a beer?”

"Sure, why not?” Kelsey said, sitting on the porch bench.

Wil came out a few moments later with two beers and a blanket. She rubbed her arms. “It gets cold out here after dark.”

He handed her the beer, took a seat, and wrapped the blanket around both of them.

"This is cozy,” she said.

The two were silent watching the sun set in the west. “This is beautiful. You’re fortunate you can see this every night.”

"Yeah, that’s true. It’s my own piece of heaven right here in South Dakota. Much different than Maryland and, I’m sure, Chicago.”

She nodded as she sipped her beer. “I actually live in Glencoe, which is the second richest suburb behind Winnetka. Glencoe sits on Lake Michigan’s northern shore and has almost nine thousand residents. The city’s crime rate is seventy-five percent below the state average, probably because the home values average almost 1.4 million dollars.”

"Wow. That’s probably a drop in the bucket for a billionaire.”

Kelsey laughed. “It sure is.”

Wil sipped on his beer. “You realize you’re the first gal who has ever spent the night here in this cabin?”

"What about Lydia or Laney?"

Wil shook his head. "Laney and I have never dated. Lydia wouldn't spend the night here; it was usually at her place in Deadwood. She was always afraid this place would blow over at the first large wind."

"Has there ever been damage because of the wind?"

"Nope. The roof has been a work in progress since I bought it two years ago. It looked much worse than it does now."

"You're telling me it's been two years, and you still don't have the roof fixed?"

Wil laughed. "Pretty close. I still have some things to fix in the bedroom, specifically over the other side of the bed."

Kelsey laughed once more.

"I love your laugh."

She peered into his eyes. "I've never laughed as much as I have with you." With a yawn, she stood up. "I should probably get some sleep. I have some Skype calls to conduct with employees tomorrow."
Kelsey reached over and kissed Wil on the cheek. "Good night and thanks for a wonderful evening."

It was an hour later when Wil finally crawled into bed. Hours later he opened his eyes, staring up at Kelsey who stood looking down at him. "I heard something I've never heard before. Can I join you?"

Wil slid over, and Kelsey crawled in front of him. He put his arms around her. "Was it the rooster?"

"A rooster. You have a rooster out here?"

"Yup, he just likes to open his beak every morning at six until someone shuts him up."

"Don't you dare."

~

Kelsey opened her eyes and peered up at Wil who was still fast asleep with his arms around her. She enjoyed having his arms around her and knew right then this was what she wanted for the rest of her life. She climbed out of bed and headed toward the shower.

Five minutes later, Kelsey screamed after turning on the water. She jumped out and wrapped her arms around herself to stop the shaking.

Wil threw open the door. "Oh," he breathed. "I should have told you after five minutes the water turns cold."

She threw her washcloth at him. "Get dressed, and I'll make us some breakfast."

Kelsey was sitting on Wil's porch bench when her cell phone rang. It was her father. Wil had already left for work.

"Kelsey, where are you?"

She stared at the phone. "I'm still in South Dakota."

"Weren't you supposed to be back today?"

"Yep."

"Are you coming back today?"

"Nope."

Kelsey could hear him grumble on the other end. "Nolan told me you broke off your engagement with him and are planning on settling down with another guy in South Dakota."

She rolled her eyes. "He must have misunderstood. I told him I had some unfinished business and would stay another week."

"What about your business?"

"I can handle it from here."

Her father's voice rose. "This is the most outlandish thing you've ever done in your life."

"Is it? I've told you and Mom I would never marry a guy unless I was in love with him, and I wasn't in love with Nolan."

"That's insane."

"Why is it insane? Maybe if you and Mom had loved each other, then you wouldn't have the issues you do."

"This is embarrassing to our family. The only thing I can do is write you out of my will."

"Then that's what you'll have to do. Are we through?"

"I can't believe you've made such a huge mistake in your life thinking about living in a state like South Dakota."

"We are through," Kelsey said, clicking off.

Chapter 10

Kelsey grabbed a beer and sat on the bench on the porch. What was she thinking? Maybe her dad was right about her dropping her life in Chicago just like that to stay with a guy she knew only a week. She couldn't help it if Wil made her feel something deep inside that she never had felt before. The reason she didn't go with him to the social was because she didn't want word to get back to Chicago for his own protection. But now it didn't matter. What if she had made a mistake? What if Wil decided he wanted nothing to do with her?

She drained a good portion of her beer, set it down, and ran her hands through her hair. What a mess. Wil was the guy she loved unconditionally. She jumped as her cell phone went off. "Wil, is that you?"

"Yeah, just wanted to let you know I'm in Custer and should be back in about an hour or more after I fill out some paperwork. I'll grab us something for supper. Anything you would like?"

"Can you grill ribs?"

"Consider it done. See you in a bit."

Kelsey shut the phone and took a deep breath. Her eyes widened when she saw a short guy staring at her from a few feet away.

"Please help me or I'll die like my brother!"

"What are you talking about?"

"Please, ma'am, they're after me, and if they find me they'll harm you also."

Kelsey jumped up off the bench and tried to help him into the cabin.

He stopped. "No ma'am, they'll look here first."

"I'll take you up into the hills a bit where there is a cave you can hide in until Wil gets back."

"Wil Bolton?"

"You know him?"

"That's who I'm looking for. My name is Alton Loe, and he saved my brother's life when he found him on a trail in Wyoming."

"This way," she said, leading him into the hills behind the cabin. Ten minutes later, she took him into a small cave that she had seen the first night she was here. "Wil should be back soon. and hopefully I'll be able to talk my way out of the situation when they show up." Kelsey hurried back down to the cabin and sat down on the porch, picking up her beer. She tried to calm herself down, wondering what was going on. How did the guy know Wil? Was she involving herself in something she couldn't get herself out of?

She took another sip of her beer hoping it would calm her down. Her eyes froze when she saw two guys coming past Box Elder Creek heading her way. She took a deep breath and waited. "Can I help you?" she asked when they approached her.

"Yeah, we're looking for a guy about five-ten, blond hair, and with a noticeable limp."

"I haven't seen anyone in these parts other than my husband."

"Is your husband here?"

"He'll be back in anytime now. He just went to grab something for supper. Actually, we're going to grill ribs tonight. I've never had them before cooked on a grill, so I'm looking forward to it." She hid shaky hands behind her.

The guys eyed her. One of the two took a step toward her. "You wouldn't be lying to us now, would you?"

"Do I look like a gal who would lie to you? If you want, check through the cabin." She climbed up and opened the door.

The other guy talked. "He can't be here, or she wouldn't let us into her cabin."

"You're right. Sorry for bothering you, ma'am."

The two hurried back down Box Elder Creek. Once they were out of sight, Kelsey dropped back down onto the bench shaking uncontrollably.

Several minutes later a deputy pulled in and jumped out of the car. "Is Wil around?"

"No sir, he should be back in a few minutes."

"Have you seen anybody come through here in the past thirty minutes?"

"Yes. Two guys just left hurrying along Box Elder Creek looking for some guy."

"Have you seen the other guy?"

Kelsey nodded. "Here, I'll show you where he is."

The deputy made a call to the sheriff's department.

"Sheriff Kanter, this is the deputy. We may have found them up at Wil's cabin near Nemo."

"On our way."

The deputy turned back to Kelsey. "Lead the way, ma'am."

In ten minutes, Kelsey showed her where Alton Loe was hiding. The deputy pulled out his pistol and pointed it at the guy who was shaking when he saw it. "Alton Loe?"

"Yes, sir. I'm Alton Loe."

"Your brother has been looking all over for you. Come with me and we'll take you back to him."

Loe looked scared. "You can't, sir. They'll kill him also."

"What are you talking about?"

Loe climbed out of the hiding place he was in, and his eyes went wide. "Drop the gun, deputy."

The deputy slowly turned around to see two men pointing guns at him. "It'd be better if you just give yourself up, Trent," he said.

"You know I can't do that. If we don't get what we're after, they'll kill us."

"What is it you're looking for?" the deputy asked.

"Drugs and money. Lots of drugs and money that our bosses want at any cost."

Alton Loe spoke up, "I don't have your drugs and money, but I know where you can find them."

The guy named Trent stared at Alton. "Oh yeah? We know you have them because your brother told us so before we shot him. That damn Bolton just happened to find him before he could bleed out, and now law enforcement knows what's going on."

Kelsey noticed the other guy staring at her. She had

seen him before, but she couldn't recall where. It would come to her. They all turned at the voice.

"Trent, drop the gun. We have you surrounded."

Trent laughed. "Sheriff Kanter, I can shoot your deputy right now. All I want is what is owed me."

The man was getting ready to pull his trigger when the other touched him. Trent whipped around to him, seeing him shake his head. Trent dropped his gun and turned to the sheriff. "You win this time, Kanter." Trent turned back to Loe. "They'll be coming for you."

The other guy nodded at Kelsey, then said just above a whisper, "Ms. Lawrence, good seeing you again."

The deputies put handcuffs on all three of them. Sheriff Kanter walked over to Kelsey. "Are you okay, Ms. Lawrence?"

She sighed. "I'm doing okay. Does this happen a lot out here?"

The sheriff shook his head. "There are criminal elements out here but nowhere near what happens in Chicago. Mostly it involves illegal drugs like what these guys are looking for."

Kelsey's brow furrowed. "Is Wil part of this?"

"Oh gosh, no. Why would you think that?"

"Because this Alton Loe knew who he was when I told him he'd be back soon."

Sheriff Kanter eyed Kelsey. "Do you believe that he is involved?"

"I don't really know what to believe right now."

"What are you doing out here?"

She took a deep breath. "I know it sounds ridiculous, but I love it here and am trying to figure out if I want to stay."

The sheriff sighed. "Have a candid talk with Wil. Once you hear what he has to say, you'll understand who he is. And ma'am, Wil is not evil. The guy is considered a hero in these Black Hills."

The deputy interrupted the conversation. "We're ready to go, Sheriff."

He nodded and turned back to Kelsey. "Wil Bolton will protect you, and you'll never have to worry about anyone harming you. You probably can't say that about your father in Chicago."

"You know my father?"

"Oh yeah, it's a safe bet your father has something to do with what is happening right here."

Chapter 11

Thirty minutes later Wil pulled into the driveway. Everyone had already left. Kelsey was sitting on the bench drinking her third beer. She was that scared about what was happening.

Wil smiled at her. "I'll fire up the grill."

Her eyes narrowed. "Who are you?"

Wil didn't answer but just turned and went over to the grill. Kelsey jumped up and hurried over to him. "I asked you a question. Who are you?"

Wil still didn't say anything but started the grill, and once it was running, he placed the ribs on it. Finally, he turned around and fixed his eyes on her. "What happened?"

"I'm here by myself, and some guy is chased to your cabin, so I take him up to a cave, then two guys show up looking for him. The deputy drives up and the two guys return and are ready to shoot all of us. Sheriff Kanter saved us. Then he said he knew my father and that he's connected somehow. But also he said I needed to listen to what you had to say about all of this."

Wil turned around and flipped over the ribs. He turned back to Kelsey's voice.

"Have I made a mistake? Please tell me so I can get out of this before anything happens to me."

"Try to calm down."

"Don't tell me to calm down, especially when a guy is pointing a gun at me, and I have no clue if I slept with a killer."

He eyed her. "You really believe I'm a killer?"

"I don't even know you, so there is that possibility."

"There's not much more to say, is there? I'll drive you to the airport as soon as I turn off the grill."

Kelsey swung him around. "No, Wil, I don't want to go to an airport. I'm in love with you, and all I'm asking is for you to tell me who you are."

"Are you sure you want to hear it?"

"I wouldn't have asked if I didn't."

He took a deep breath. "I brought some barbecue sauce for the ribs, so why don't you grab it, along with potato salad and baked beans, and we'll talk while we eat."

"I'm not hungry," she said.

Wil grinned. "You should really try these before you say that." He cut off a piece and fed her a bite.

"Wow, maybe you're right." Kelsey grabbed the rest of the food out of the refrigerator while Wil plated the ribs and set them on the table. She joined him with the rest of the food a minute later.

"These are very good," Kelsey said, taking her first bite.

Wil nodded and turned to her. "I left Maryland

after my parents were killed in a car crash. I attended Frostburg State University in Maryland and earned a degree in wildlife biology. My first job offer was right here in the Black Hills National Forest as one of its wildlife biologists." He sighed. "It never happened because the position was cut, but Mr. Hampton hired me anyway to chase down animal tracks and provide tourists with an experience in the Black Hills. The truth is, I love the outdoors because it's the only place I feel any peace, and that's why I live out here in this cabin even as junky as it is."

The two gnawed on their ribs, reaching over to dab at barbecue sauce on their cheeks. "I told you the truth when I said I wanted to chase down treasures, but I don't know if that will ever happen. As for today, I knew nothing about what went on, but I do know that there are plenty of drugs that flow through the Black Hills every day. I've run across druggies several times while touring with others in the Black Hills."

Kelsey finally spoke. "I'm not naive enough to know that those things don't occur, but what happened today scared me to death, and you weren't here to protect me. I don't know if I can deal with being out in the boonies without protection. At least I have that in my father's mansion and at my work in Chicago."

Wil eyed her. "Did you truly believe that nothing like this wouldn't happen in South Dakota?"

"Not like it does in Chicago, and that's a big reason why I wanted to stay here. I don't want to worry about criminal elements, and I sure don't want our children to be subject to something like that."

He did a doubletake before he shrugged. "I'll take you to the airport in the morning."

She took her plate and went into the cabin. From the window she could see Wil cleaning the grill then he sat down on the porch with a beer. An hour later Kelsey came out and sat down next to him. She took his hands. "I don't want to leave here, and I want to spend my life with you, but it really scared me what happened today."

He reached over and put his arm around her shoulders. She snuggled into him. "I don't blame you," he said. "But then again, I don't know what you were expecting from me. You tell me you've fallen in love with me, and I can't understand how that can be in such a short period of time knowing nothing about me."

She peered into his eyes. "How do you feel about me?"

"I feel the same way about you."

"You don't know me, and when I told you I was rich you hardly blinked. Why didn't you feel anything?"

Wil sipped his beer. "I just knew I loved everything about you, and I didn't care if you were rich, poor, or anything else. You're the gal I've always been looking for and wasn't sure I would ever find. I guess I was right because once you found out who I was, it changed how you felt about me."

Kelsey squeezed his hands. "I told you it scared me, and I didn't know how to deal with it. I'm not sure about anything right now."

"I'll take you to the airport in the morning."

~

Wil sat on the bench for another couple of hours. It was around midnight when he walked into the cabin. He quietly walked by the bedroom Kelsey was sleeping in and heard her crying. He climbed into his bed and fell asleep immediately. Hours later Wil felt someone standing over him. He opened one eye at a time. "What are you doing?"

Kelsey sat down on the bed beside him and reached down and kissed him gently on the lips. "I'm not going anywhere. You're the guy I love and want to be with me no matter where this life takes us."

Wil sat up, and she crawled onto his lap and put her arms around him. He peered into her eyes. "What I did in my past is over with. If all I have is you and a family, I'm cool with that."

She kissed him once more. "That's all I've ever wanted despite what my family wants from me. I don't want to go to the Rapid City Airport. What I want is to spend my life with you and raise a family. I hope you feel the same way."

Chapter 12

Wil sat on the bench on the front porch of the cabin eating pancakes and drinking coffee. Kelsey joined him with her breakfast.

"Most normal people sit at a kitchen table when they eat meals."

He pointed. "Then you wouldn't be able to see that."

"Are those turkeys?"

"Wild turkeys. I've seen them but not that many at one time."

Her hand went to her chest. "Wow, you're right. This is much better than eating at the table." She turned toward him. "Are we okay?"

He kissed her on the forehead. "We're all right. What happened yesterday is over with."

"How can you just forget something so quickly?"

"You learn how to get over things when you lose your parents."

"I'm sorry."

He shook his head. "Don't be. My life is looking much better now."

She grinned. "I hope so. Remember when I told you if I fell in love with you, you'd never get rid of me?"

"You did say that. I had hoped, but I didn't know what to expect."

Kelsey finished chewing a portion of her pancake. "If yesterday is any indication, our life is never going to be dull."

"One thing I've been thinking about was when you mentioned the sheriff knew your father. What do you think that meant?"

Kelsey shrugged. "I can't answer that, but I do know that my father and uncle are involved with many schemes, so there is a chance they're involved in some shady dealings. My dad is pretty pissed at me for leaving Chicago and chasing down a guy I hardly know. I don't care." She sipped her coffee. "It's kind of strange that I would connect with a guy who probably doesn't make fifty thousand dollars a year and love him."

Wil laughed. "It's probably because I'm so classy."

Kelsey laughed. "I've never laughed or blushed as much with any guy as I have with you." She took a deep breath. "There's something you need to know about me. My father, mother, brother, and sister all have had extramarital affairs, and I was afraid I would do the same thing. I know that won't happen because you're the only guy I ever think about, which is insane. When I was dating Clinton, I was thinking about Nolan, and when I was dating Nolan, I was thinking about another guy, and so on and so on."

"Wow, I really don't need to hear this."

She eyed him. "I wanted to tell you that was who I was, but I'm not that girl anymore, nor do I want to be. It's the same as you. What about your love life?"

"Lydia was special in my life, but I did have two gals I dated earlier. Nothing came of either one of them, which is probably good."

"Why?"

Wil sighed. "I didn't have enough money."

Kelsey laughed, spitting out the pancake piece she had in her mouth.

They both turned when a limousine pulled into the driveway. The limo stopped, and a tall guy stepped out. He had a tailored beard, short haircut, and wore glasses. "Are you Wil Bolton?"

"It depends on who's asking," Wil said.

The guy laughed. "Quite an introduction, and I'm sorry about that. I'm Boris Loe, and I wanted to thank you for saving my two brothers' lives. May I join you?"

"Sure, have a seat."

Kelsey stood up. "Would you like some coffee?"

"I'd love some."

Kelsey hurried in and brought out a chair for Mr. Loe to sit in.

"Thank you," he smiled.

She went back in and came out with a cup of coffee. "I bought a couple of sugars and a creamer if you would like that."

"I'd love it," he said, stirring his coffee. He handed the creamer back to Kelsey who hurried back into the house with it.

Once out she sat down next to Wil. "Oh, I'm sorry. I can leave you two to talk."

"No, Ms. Lawrence, you're more than welcome to join us."

"How do you know who I am?"

"My brother, Alton, told me about you, but even if he didn't, I would have known you because your face is in several magazines around Chicago."

"You're from Chicago?" Wil asked.

"I am and have had dealings with Kelsey's family. In particular, Andy and Ben, both of whom I'm not happy to have dealt with. I'm sorry about that, Ms. Lawrence."

"Don't be. I've had a hard time with them also."

Loe sipped on his coffee. "The reason I stopped by here is to talk to you about my company, and what we're hoping to accomplish in the future. Loe Enterprises is a construction and engineering company with worldwide implications. We're interested in expanding our business portfolio to hunt treasures around the world. Have you heard of Treasure Paradise?"

Wil shook his head, but Kelsey nodded. "Isn't that a project involving my family and Dr. Isaac Regret?"

"It was, but this past week, Dr. Regret contacted me and asked me to take the project over because of some health issues within his family. I bought the rights to the entity for three million dollars, and Dr. Regret will receive a percentage of any proceeds we should earn in the process."

"What about my family?" Kelsey asked.

"They had their chance to buy it but chose not to because they have decided to start their own thing. This means we'll be competing for the same treasures around the world. Of course, there are many others who are searching for these items each day."

Wil took a drink of his coffee and spoke, "What do I have to do with it?"

"I've heard about some of the things you've accomplished just in the last year. You saved my brother's life after a bullet wound, took down a mountain lion in full stride, and brought a group of hikers out of the hills after dark. I want you to develop strategies and lead my group to find these treasures." He sipped on his coffee. "You work for the Black Hills National Forest, but I will pay you handsomely for what you'll be doing with me with full benefits, and you'll be able to continue living in your rustic cabin right here."

"It's something I've always thought about, but my circumstances have changed in the past few weeks."

"Ah, Ms. Lawrence. I understand. How about I leave you my card, and you think about it for the next few days? Call me either way on Friday?"

Wil took Mr. Loe's card.

"Ms. Lawrence, it was wonderful meeting you and Mr. Bolton, and I hope to talk to you once more."

Once he left, Kelsey looked at him. "It's what you've always wanted to do. Why are you hesitant?"

"For several reasons. One is he's involved with a guy who almost sent me to a Mexican prison for several years. And what happened to Dr. Regret that he would turn his project over to Mr. Loe and not your family? And what about us?"

"What about us?"

"I want to build a relationship with you, and a proposition like his doesn't help that at all. How are you going to handle me flying around the world all the time?"

She took his hands. "You have no reason to believe me because we've only known each other for a week, but believe me when I tell you that you're the guy I'll always be waiting for, and no other guy will ever touch my heart like you have. This is something you've always wanted, and I'll support you as much as I can."

"I don't know, but I should get to work."

She framed her hands gently around his face and kissed his lips. "That will always be waiting for you, to keep you coming home from wherever you are."

Chapter 13

Kelsey grabbed another cup of coffee and positioned her laptop out on the porch. She set up a Skype with members of her clothing and design board. They needed to discuss upcoming trips to Asia and South America.

It was eleven when she contacted her board in Chicago. They usually met for a board meeting at eleven and then had lunch before continuing with their day.

"Good morning, Gemini," Kelsey said. Gemini Jones was Kelsey's administrative assistant and also one of her closest friends. The two had been friends since grade school.

"Hi, Kelsey. How is South Dakota?"

"It's beautiful. I have a rooster that wakes me up at six every morning, and I've seen a bear, wild turkeys, deer, and a mountain lion."

"It's like you have your own zoo. How's the guy you're chasing?"

"Wonderful. We've had many detailed conversations, and we've not slept together yet, which I'm happy about. Do you know anything about what's happening with Dr. Regret and my family?"

"Yeah, your father was pretty ticked off when he found out that a judge said Dr. Regret had the copyright for the Treasure Paradise brand. Your father decided to drop out because he wanted nothing to do with it if he couldn't have it all. Now, he's working with another group to come up with some other kind of treasure-hunting venture. Stay tuned."

Kelsey took a deep breath. "They'll get what they want."

"The board is coming into the room as we speak."

"Great. Let's get started."

Kelsey joined the zoom group. "Good morning. I hope things are going well for you in Chicago."

Board President Kenneth Walker did the talking for the board. "Kelsey, are you enjoying your time in South Dakota? Is it going to be permanent?"

"I'm loving it here, and I'll find out by the end of the week if this will be a permanent home for me. We'll see. I've received some information regarding Roberto Santiago and a clothing or textile company in Rio De Janeiro. Have you all received that information?"

"We have," Walker said.

"Your initial thoughts?" Kelsey asked.

"I've had a simple conversation with Santiago this past week, and he's interested in a group of us joining him in Brazil next month. Your thoughts?"

"I'll coordinate with him and see what we can arrange. Let me know which board members can make it and some dates you'd be available to fly there. The information provided will open up a different market for us—more low-end prices than what we're used to."

Over the next thirty minutes, the board discussed the budget. Kelsey found out that most areas of the business were growing except for Budapest, Hungary.

"Do you have any idea what the problem is in that area?" Walker asked.

"Initial indications show that there are a couple of new clothing companies that have opened up in the area, so competition is high. That's why it's important to find other markets," Kelsey explained. "Along with South America, I've had some discussions with Asian markets, in particular the islands in the South Pacific, and Australia and New Zealand."

"Any luck?" Walker asked.

"I've had good initial contacts with a couple of companies in Australia and Micronesia, as well as the Melanesia islands in the South Pacific. Another possibility is Papua New Guinea."

"What are your thoughts, Kelsey?" Chet asked.

"Let's focus on Brazil for sure and then Australia and Papua New Guinea. Those are the two Pacific area countries that seem to have the most interest. We'll plan on sending a group to meet with the leaders in those areas over the next six months."

After several other questions, the board broke for lunch. Before Gemini shut down, Kelsey asked her to call back to discuss what the next steps would be. Since she couldn't join them for lunch, Kelsey made herself a sandwich, her eyes taking in the cabin's main room. What could be done with it to make it more habitable?

They would have to expand the cabin and add more bedrooms because she planned to have children with

Wil. At least she was hoping he would be agreeable to raising a family. She took a bite of her sandwich, reflecting on what needed to be done first. For sure, the roof needed to be completed, they would need a new refrigerator and stove, and a new bathroom. The outhouse was going by the wayside immediately.

How would they pay for everything? Kelsey could dip into her own account to take care of it all, but she had a feeling Wil would want to handle it himself, which brought a smile to her face. A refreshing change since most guys always mooched off her or her family.

~

Wil was driving down Highway 385 when his cell phone vibrated. He pulled over and answered it.

The name of one of the weekend dispatchers at the forest service popped up. "Wil, we have an issue near Ditch Creek. A guy claims to have shot a mountain lion who was seen in the area."

"I'm on my way." Wil drove toward Ditch Creek in the southern part of the forest. He arrived an hour later and pulled up to a cabin.

The owner was waiting for him. "It was a mountain lion. I know I hit it. It's over there in that area of the forest."

Wil stared at the man. "You had to shoot it?"

"I was protecting myself."

"Where is it?"

"Follow me."

The two walked about three hundred feet when they saw the mountain lion lying on the ground. It was still breathing but was bleeding badly. Wil raised his rifle and shot a tranquilizer into him. It knocked him out quickly.

Wil went to get his pickup and backed it up to the mountain lion. "Here, help me put him in the back of the pickup. He's asleep and he won't move."

The two hoisted the mountain lion into the back of the truck. Wil sped down the road toward Custer. He contacted the forest service to let them know he had the lion. They said they would call a local veterinarian to handle the wound in Custer. Forty minutes later Wil rolled into Custer and straight to the vet. He and a member of Game, Fish, and Parks were waiting for him. They unloaded him and Wil filled out a report. He drove back toward his cabin arriving around six.

When Wil strolled through the front door, Kelsey turned toward him smiling. "Just in time for supper."

He stared at her. "How were you able to figure out the stove?"

"Easy. I'm not just a rich girl; I do have cooking skills. Go change, and let's eat some spaghetti with garlic toast."

He came out of the bedroom and went to the kitchen. "What do you want to drink?" she asked.

"Iced tea tonight."

"Two iced teas coming up. I'll bring it out to you at our favorite spot."

Wil sat down and stared out at the emptiness. Kelsey came out a few moments later with a plate of spaghetti, garlic toast on the side, and iced tea. She joined him a minute later. "Well, how does it taste?" she asked, flopping down next to him.

"I was waiting for you."

"How sweet."

The two dug into their supper. Wil gazed at her. "This is wonderful."

She giggled. "I'm so happy. Spaghetti is one of my favorite meals, and it was the first dish I wanted to cook for you. There is this misconception that rich people have someone do all their cooking for them. It isn't a misconception in our family, but I always wanted to cook for the guy I'm with. Of course, you're the first guy I've ever cooked for, so that in itself means a lot to me."

"How did your meeting go today?" Wil asked.

"Great. I'll be traveling to Brazil in the next month and then to the South Pacific Islands in the next six months for some possible new contracts."

"Good for you. That has to be exciting."

She looked astonished. "It doesn't bother you?"

He shook his head. "Why would it? It's part of your job."

"You continue to amaze me because every guy I've dated wouldn't agree to something like this and would do what they could to make me feel guilty."

Wil grinned. "Someday I'll need you to feel the same way when I go galivanting around the world looking for treasures."

"You've decided to take Mr. Loe up on his job offer?"

"I'm thinking about it but wanted to talk to you about it."

She grinned. "Does that mean you want me in your life?"

"Thought that was a foregone conclusion. I'm sure you have this cabin already redecorated, room additions, etc."

She laughed. "How did you know?"

"Just had a feeling."

"How was your day?"

Wil finished eating a forkful of spaghetti before answering. "I helped a cabin owner haul in a mountain lion he had shot."

"Did he kill it?" Kelsey's eyes widened.

"No, he wounded it. I tranquilized it and carried it back to a vet in Custer. The mountain lion should be okay."

"What happened to the guy who shot it?"

"Usually nothing because he was defending his property and wasn't actively hunting the mountain lion. If he was hunting the lion, then he would be charged."

Wil finished his drink. "Feel like going gambling with me?"

"What? I didn't think you liked to gamble."

"I don't, but Laney and Amanda invited us to join them and their other halves for a night of gambling."

"I'd love to. Let me change into something nice."

Chapter 14

Wil and Kelsey walked into Ben Franklin Hotel. Once a month on Tuesdays a group of friends got together and gambled until they lost the amount they started with. For most it was one hundred dollars.

"Will you look at this? Wil Bolton is joining us," Caleb said.

"And with a date," Bailey added.

Everyone laughed at Wil blushing. "I'm here because of Kelsey."

Kelsey stuck her arm into his. "I'm excited to do something with Wil and his friends."

"When are you two getting married?" Laney grinned.

"Who said anything about marriage? I don't even know if she's going to stay here."

Kelsey winked at Laney. "All he has to do is ask me, and I'll marry him in a heartbeat."

Everyone laughed once more at Wil blushing.

Wil waved a dismissive hand. "Let's do this

gambling before I change my mind."

Caleb explained the rules. "We all set the amount we're going to gamble, and the one who wins the most money tonight gets a free ride next month. It means everyone has to chip in and provide that person the amount to gamble with."

Wil grinned. "So basically, if I win each month with the most money, I won't have to spend one cent of my own."

Bailey nodded. "You got it, but it'll never happen because we've been doing this for six months, and not once has anyone won two months in a row. Unless you have a system."

Wil rolled his eyes. "It's simple. I'll let Laney or Amanda stick all their money in, and then I'll follow right behind them and clean up."

"Sorry, Wil, that would be considered cheating," Kelsey said. "You have to do your own thing."

Caleb laughed. "I like this girl already. Are you sure you wouldn't consider dating me and dumping Wil?"

Kelsey shook her head. "Won't ever happen."

The group went on their way for the next ninety minutes and wound up at the Old Style Number Ten Saloon to add up their winnings. When it was finished, Wil wound up with the most money with more than two hundred dollars, and Laney lost fifty-seven dollars.

They all sat back at a corner table with drinks. Wil leaned back in his chair. "This gambling thing isn't so bad."

Bailey smirked. "Beginners luck, I'm sure."

"I just know if I come back next month, I won't have to pay for my gambling."

Kelsey eyed him. "We are coming back next month, Wil, and every month after as long as we're here."

Everyone else snickered.

Wil and Kelsey arrived back at the cabin after ten then sat on the bench on the porch.

"That was so much fun. I'm glad we went," Kelsey said.

"I did have fun, but mostly because you were with me."

She eyed him and then jumped up and hurried into the cabin. She came out with a blanket, sat down next to Wil, and wrapped the blanket around the two of them. "You're right, it does get cold out here."

He put his arm around her, and she snuggled into him, resting her head on his shoulder while they peered into the sky. Kelsey finally spoke. "I loved studying science in school, and I was especially into astronomy, but I couldn't tell you any of the constellations at this time."

Wil pointed up into the stars. "You can tell that's the big dipper because it has seven bright stars with four looking like a bowl and the other three looking like a handle. And not too far away is the little dipper."

"Wow, I can see them both as clear as day tonight."

Both were quiet for the next fifteen minutes staring up in the sky. Finally, Kelsey pulled her blanket off her. "I'm heading to bed. Thank you for another wonderful evening. Good night."

Wil sat out for another hour and finally climbed into bed around eleven-thirty. He woke up as usual around six when he heard the rooster. Kelsey joined him and he moved over so she could climb into the bed. "You know you can sleep right here with me, so you don't have to worry about the rooster."

She observed him. "I'm not ready yet, but it'll happen soon, and then you'll never get me out of your bed."

They both had just fallen asleep again when Wil's radio started squawking. "Wil, are you there?"

Wil jumped out of bed and hurried to the microphone. "I'm right here."

"A lightning strike hit an area around where that major Jasper fire was in 2000," Forest-Service Manager Hampton said. "Bailey is on his way with a chopper. There is a family who can't get out of there and need help."

Wil rushed into the bedroom and started to get dressed.

"Is everything okay?"

"A lightning strike in an area west of Custer. Bailey is on his way."

She jumped out of bed and held him tightly. "Please be careful, and come back as soon as you can."

"I don't know how long it will be, but Amanda or Laney will make sure you're aware of what's happening."

"They would do that?" she asked.

Wil nodded. "We've all been friends for the last couple of years, and you are one of us now. Try not to worry."

"I don't know how I'm going to be able to do that."

He took her face gently and kissed her solidly on the lips. She peered into his eyes. "I'll be right here waiting for you."

Twenty minutes later, Bailey landed in a patch of grass outside the cabin. Wil climbed in, and they lifted back up into the air and headed toward Custer.

"It's bad," Caleb said. "There is an elderly man and his granddaughter in the middle of the fire, and they can't get out. Firefighters are out there as we speak, but the fire took off quickly because everything is so dry out there."

"How do they plan to rescue them?" Wil asked.

"We have no clue right now," Bailey said as they sped toward the fire.

Wil took a deep breath. "Do you know where they are?"

"We have a general location."

"Okay, then drop me into it, and we'll lift them out of the air."

Bailey and Caleb both stared at him. "Are you crazy? You'll burn alive," Caleb said.

"Do you have a better idea?"

"No, but that's suicide," Bailey said.

"Not with you flying. We can do this."

Caleb radioed back to the forest-service headquarters to let them know what was about to happen. Hampton got on the phone and squelched the idea.

Wil took the microphone. "Boss, if we don't do anything right now, they'll burn alive because the firefighters can't reach them fast enough. Bailey can hover above long enough for me to hook them up and get them out. It'll take a couple of times, but it can be done."

Hampton sighed. "Wil, we've never done anything like this before."

"We've swung from the helicopter in the past, and if we don't do it now, who knows what will happen to the family. We'll be okay."

After a moment or so, Hampton finally gave in. Bailey headed toward the last known sight of the two people. All the others had gotten out okay.

Caleb turned and stared at Wil. "You've never done this, have you?"

Wil shook his head. "We have to try something."

Bailey hovered above the last location where the two people were. "There's the cabin right below us." As soon as Caleb hooked Wil to a rope, he slid down to just outside the cabin. A young girl opened the door as soon as he landed.

"Please help my grandpa. I think he had a heart attack, and he's having a hard time breathing."

Wil hurried in and checked the pulse of the guy. He radioed Caleb. "We need the stretcher. The old man is barely breathing. It looks like he's had a heart attack."

"Got it."

Wil gently lifted the man and carried him. "Please open the door."

The girl did as he asked. A stretcher was lowered down, and Wil hooked him up tightly and tugged on the rope signaling them to pull the man up. "We'll take care of him."

Wil looked around as the fire was getting closer. They both stared up as they lifted her grandfather up to the chopper. A few moments later the rope slid back down. Wil grabbed it. "Hold on tightly to my back, and they'll lift us up into the chopper."

They started to go up, but just like that, the wind blew some fire onto the rope just above them and Wil had to drop to the ground with the girl falling on him. He grabbed her and rolled just as a tree came down. Wil lifted her up and raced toward an open area.

He pushed the radio. "Get him out of here."

"We can't leave you, Wil," Caleb said.

"Go. The fire is too much, and Bailey won't be able to handle the chopper. The guy needs help. I'll get his granddaughter out of here."

"Damn it, Wil," Caleb said.

Wil shut off his phone and took off with the young girl away from the fire. They reached a place out of the fire's reach and watched as the chopper lifted up and sped off.

"We'll find a way out," Wil said.

Chapter 15

Kelsey was cleaning around the cabin when she heard a vehicle flying toward the cabin. She opened the door and stepped outside. Laney jumped out of the car and ran over to her, tears flowing down her cheeks.

"What happened?"

"We don't know if Wil's alive."

Kelsey's mouth dropped. "What do you mean?"

"We have to go. I'm taking you to the fire-command center. He's lost somewhere in the middle of the fire, which is getting larger as we speak."

Kelsey hurried back into the cabin and grabbed a couple of personal items. "I'm ready."

Laney sped toward the command center just west of Custer, and they arrived an hour later. Laney pulled into a parking area, the gals jumped out, and hurried over to a large tent. Bailey and Caleb were both standing there when they came in.

Bailey hurried over and hugged Laney. "Any word?" she asked.

"Nothing. We've lost all contact with him and the little girl. Worse yet, the firefighters can't get to that area because of the terrain and the heat of the fire."

"What's happening?" Kelsey asked.

Bailey took Kelsey's hand and took her outside to explain to her. "We lowered Wil down into the middle of the fire right next to a cabin. An old man and young girl were trapped, and the old man had a heart attack. We were able to lift the man to safety and were pulling Wil and the young girl up, but the wind pushed fire toward the rope burning it just above where Wil was climbing, and they fell to the ground."

Kelsey covered her mouth. "Is he alive?"

"He was the last we saw of him. He took the girl, and they raced into the forest away from the fire, but we haven't heard from him since, and that's been a couple of hours now."

"What are they doing to find them?"

"There's nothing we can do right now because the fire is too hot at that spot. The only good thing about this is that Wil knows the Black Hills like the back of his hand. If there's a way out, he'll find it."

~

Wil and the young girl made their way to water where they were able to dive in away from the fire.

"What will happen to Grandpa?" she asked.

"I don't know. We'll find out as soon as we get out of here."

"My grandpa said we would die in the forest from a fire one of these days."

"What is your name?"

"Aubrey, and I'm thirteen."

"Where's your mom and dad?"

"They died a year ago, and I moved out here with him because I had nowhere else to go. They were going to put me in social services unless he took me. At times he didn't want me."

Wil took the girl's hand. "Are you ready to move? We have to find a way out of the fire."

"It is hot."

The two continued to trek to the west. The fire continued to surround them as they made their way trying to find a place to escape the fire. After about an hour, Wil and the young girl stopped for a break.

"Where are we?" Aubrey asked.

"We're deep in the national forest, and there is nothing in the area. I'm trying to find a cave or something where we can spend the night."

The young girl wiped her face with her fists. "The smoke is hurting my eyes."

Wil searched the area and thought he saw a glint or something shiny like a group of rocks. He lifted the girl up into his arms. "Cover your eyes with the shirt on my shoulder."

She did as he asked, and they headed toward the rocks. After about fifteen minutes, Wil reached the rocks, and he was right about a cave of sorts. He pushed away some weeds and slowly climbed into the area. There was enough space where the two could wait out the night. In addition, he heard a small waterfall.

"Aubrey, it looks like we've found a place out of the smoke for the evening." He set her down and grabbed some twigs and branches and whatever else he could find to start a fire to keep them warm for the evening. Once he got it started, he took a canteen out of his backpack and placed it under the waterfall for water. "Here you go, little lady. Drink slowly."

Once she finished, she looked at him. "I'm

hungry."

Wil pulled out a couple of bars out of his backpack. "This will have to do for the moment."

"What are they?"

"Protein bars. I eat them when I'm out in the forest because it helps me keep my strength up."

Aubrey opened the wrapper and slowly ate the bar. She looked at Wil who was trying to make some kind of bed for her to sleep on. "Will we get out of here, or will I die in a fire like Grandpa said?"

"Aubrey, we're going to do everything we can to make it out alive." Once he finished making Aubrey a bed, he sat down by her and ate his protein bar. "Where do you go to school?"

"I'm a seventh-grade student at Custer Middle School. The bus comes all the way out to my grandpa's place to pick me up. Sometimes it gets really hard for it to get there."

"Where did you live before?"

"Mom and Dad had a house in Hot Springs before that. I also had a little brother who died in the car crash."

"You weren't with them?"

"No, I had spent the night at my friend's house. I haven't seen her since."

"I'm sorry. How about you lie down here and try to get some sleep? I'll stay up until you're finished sleeping, and then we'll figure out what to do in the morning. The cave should help."

"Thank you for saving my grandpa."

"You're welcome. You'll be seeing him soon."

She lay down and gazed at Wil. "I don't think so."

~

Kelsey was sitting on a rock by herself looking toward the west, seeing the smoke from the fire. Laney came over and sat with her.

"What was Wil thinking when he dropped into the middle of a fire?" Kelsey asked.

"All he was thinking about was saving them. Nothing else."

"He does live an adventurous life, and I don't know how anyone can deal with it."

Laney didn't say anything for a moment. "Kelsey, he does care about you immensely."

"And I care about him, also. I told him I would stay an extra week because I had some unfinished business to attend to, and it was him. Twice now I've been scared out of my wits from something associated with him. The first was when someone pointed a gun at me and now this. I don't know if I can deal with this. I had hoped I could, but I don't think it's possible."

Laney hugged Kelsey. "Wil is hard to understand at times, but he'll never let anything happen to you."

"I believe that, but I don't think he'll stop taking all these chances with his life. It's hard to sit home and worry about whether or not he'll come back alive."

"Don't think like that. He'll be fine."

Kelsey blew out her breath. "Since I was seventeen, my father has tried to decide who I should marry and who I should associate with. Not once has he taken into consideration how I feel about the guy I want to marry. I truly love Wil, and for the first time in my life, I'm going to find a way to build a relationship with him instead of leaving when it gets tough."

"Good for you. You won't regret it."

Chapter 16

Wil slept against the cave wall when the sun started to peek out of the sky. Aubrey was still sleeping. He slid up the wall and stepped toward the cave opening to see what was happening. The fire was still going strong. Wil turned to a noise and saw Aubrey was stirring.

"Is the fire finished?"

"Nope. We'll have to hightail it out of here."

They hurried down a trail away from the smoke. Wil had placed cloths around their mouths and noses to keep the smoke out. They had travelled for an hour when Wil took a break.

"Do you think my grandpa is okay?"

"We have to hope for the best."

They continued walking on the trail but came to an area where they couldn't get around because a tree had fallen over, and they couldn't crawl over it.

"We'll have to go over the hill there."

"What if there's a fire on the other side of the hill?"

"We'll deal with it then." Wil bent down. "Climb onto my back and hold on tightly around my neck because we'll be climbing higher over the hill."

Aubrey did as Wil asked, and the two started the climb. The fire seemed to be gaining on them as they climbed the hill. They finally made it to the top, and Wil took a deep breath. He surveyed the area and found no fire on that side of the hill.

The two slowly made their way down the hill and made it down two hours later. Wil took another break and reached into his backpack. "Here, sip on this water and eat one of these protein bars."

She smiled as she chewed. "I never knew these protein bars could be this good, and they're providing me some energy."

"We'll need it because we still have a ways to go yet."

"Are we out of the fire?"

"The fire is on the other side of the hill, but that doesn't mean it can't jump over it. We have to keep moving."

The duo spent the afternoon traveling to the west toward Vestal Springs, an unincorporated town that Wil had visited once. There wasn't much there, but it would provide them with a safe haven for the evening. Wil stopped midway through the afternoon and looked back toward the fire. He was correct—the fire had jumped the hills behind them and was heating up toward them.

"It's coming after us, isn't it?" Aubrey asked.

"It sure does look that way. We should move. Climb on my back once more."

She did allow Wil to move quicker down the trail. It was almost dark when they came into Vestal Springs.

The town was vacant, and Wil looked to the west to find out the reason why. Another fire had started in that direction, and the small town was right in the middle.

Wil and Aubrey settled down in a vacant bar for the night. There happened to be chips, sandwiches, and drinks, which was convenient because the two were hungry.

"I've always liked barbecue chips, but I haven't had any for a long time," Aubrey said.

Wil reached over and grabbed the chips. "Here you go."

"Are you just stealing them?"

"No, we'll pay for everything we take here. How about a sandwich? What do you want to drink?"

"I would like a sandwich and maybe a Coke, if that's okay?"

"Sure enough." Wil grabbed those and a sandwich and Coke for himself. The two sat at a table and started eating their food.

"Are there a lot of fires in the Black Hills?" Aubrey asked.

Wil munched on his chips giving him time to think about what he wanted to say. "In the last thirty years, the national forest has averaged ninety-nine fires per year that burned more than seventy-nine hundred acres. It is estimated that seventy-five percent started from lightning strikes, with the rest coming from humans."

"That's a lot of fires."

"It is. The Jasper fire, which is near the area where this fire started, was the largest fire in 2000. I believe more than 83,000 acres burned."

"You know a lot about fires."

"I've spent the last couple of years in the forest,

and I love history. What are you interested in?"

"I like the outdoors, but I also like reading and animals. Do you have a girlfriend?"

"I'm not quite sure."

"What does that mean?"

"I do like one gal, but I'm not sure how she really feels. We're a work in progress."

"I don't have a boyfriend yet, and I'm not sure if I want one."

"You're a little young to worry about a boyfriend right now."

"That's true, but I'm sure that someday I'll like some boy, and I just hope some boy likes me."

"Believe me, Aubrey, some boy is going to like you." The next morning Wil was up just as the sun was rising. He looked out the door and noticed the fire had gained some momentum over the evening and was bearing down on them. He quickly loaded some food and water into his backpack and shook Aubrey.
"Let's go. The fire is getting closer."

She jumped up, and the two headed north toward Crazy Horse Monument. Later in the morning, they saw the carving on the side of the mountain, but the fire had surrounded them.

"I think we're close to getting help. Climb onto my back and wrap this around your mouth and eyes." He did the same thing with the cloth that he had. "Hold on because this is going to be tough."

Over the next fifteen minutes, the two struggled through the fire. Wil was hoping to make it to the monument where there would be help. The smoke was making it more difficult to breathe, but just like that they stepped out onto Highway 85 as a car flew by. Wil pulled Aubrey away, and they both rolled down into the ditch.

Chapter 17

Wil opened his eyes, and the first person he saw was Kelsey. "Where am I?"

"Rapid City Monument Hospital. The doctor said you'll be okay, and you've suffered smoke inhalation because of the forest fire. The good news is that they put the fire out just yesterday."

"What about Aubrey?"

"Is that the little girl who was with you?"

Wil nodded.

"She was released yesterday to social services."

"Aw. That's too bad. That's the last thing she wanted. What day is it?"

"Friday."

"That means you'll be heading back to Chicago tomorrow."

"I don't think so. I decided to wait another week to see where we're going with our relationship. The truth is, I'll probably stick around here much longer if you want me in your life."

"I didn't think you'd want to be after what happened."

"I thought about it, but my heart told me you're the guy I want to spend my life with, and I'll be able to deal with your adventurous spirit."

"You'd be the first."

She laughed. "Just don't disappoint me."

"What do you mean by that?"

"I can't believe I said that, but every guy I've ever cared about did something to break off the relationship – slept with other women, drank too much, or even decided to leave in the middle of the night."

"That wouldn't be me. I care a lot about you."

"They did too, but in the end it wasn't enough."

He eyed her. "I'm not like any other guy."

"I've noticed that."

They both turned to the voice of the doctor who walked in. "Wil, everything is looking good, so we can release you from the hospital. If you have any lingering effects, please contact someone immediately."

"I'll make sure he does that," Kelsey said.

It was just before lunch when the duo left the hospital. Kelsey drove Wil's pickup truck. "Are you hungry?" she asked.

"Anything's better than hospital food. I know a gal who enjoys tacos. How about that?"

"A man after my own heart."

The two drove to a taco joint on the outskirts of Rapid City. They ordered their meal and sat at a table. "What is it with you and tacos?" Wil asked.

"I'm not sure. I had one in the Rapid City Mall, and it tasted good. I've never had any in Chicago. The food we usually ate was shrimp, oysters, and other stuff like that. I've enjoyed the tacos and especially the brats we had the other night. You're corrupting me."

Wil laughed. "I'm still pinching myself trying to figure out if this is real."

"What do you mean?"

"You're a rich and beautiful gal, and you can have anything you want. I live in an old, rustic cabin in the middle of nowhere."

She reached over and grabbed his hands. "I'll explain it the best I can. I was raised in a rich world and dated guys who also had lots of money. I hosted and attended fancy parties, dressed in expensive clothes, and enjoyed fancy cars. My family always pushed me toward marrying someone rich. The moment I saw your midnight blue eyes and handsome, rugged face, that all changed. All I could see was a guy I could fall in love with."

She stopped talking when their tacos were brought to them. "The truth is, I'm scared, and I don't know how to deal with you and me. I've never cooked for any guy nor would I. Before I met you, when I dated a guy, I always thought about other men. I haven't thought about one other guy since I've seen you."

Both were silent as they finished their meal. Kelsey gazed up at Wil. "Needless to say, you've rocked my world, and I don't know how to handle it, but I'll find a way to deal with it because I do love you with all my heart."

Wil finished eating his taco. "I had always thought I would never find a gal who loved me for me, and that's the main reason I came to South Dakota and bought a rundown cabin—to get away from everyone and everything. I love it out here in the forest because it's so peaceful and beautiful. It was fair to say the gal I'd meet and fall in love with wouldn't be able to handle the loneliness, and I'm hesitant about the two of us because this is a totally different world than you've ever been involved with."

"That's true," she said, slurping her drink. "The difference is you're in my world, and I will treasure living here in the sticks and waiting for you to come back from your adventures just to be with you. You're the guy I've always dreamed of, and I'm not going to lose you."

On the way back to Nemo, Wil received a call from Bailey asking them to join them on a weekend camping trip near Deerfield Lake. He looked over at Kelsey and asked her what she thought.

"I'd love it, Wil."

Wil relayed the message to Bailey. "We'll be joining you."

~

Wil and Kelsey sat in the backseat of Bailey's car as they headed toward Deerfield Lake Resort and Campground on Friday night. Laney read a brochure that listed what was in the cabins they would be spending the weekend in.

"Each cabin has two queen-sized beds, a private bathroom with a standing shower, and an open floor plan with a kitchenette area."

Bailey laughed. "Wow, all the comforts of home."

Laney lightly smacked him. "Quit being a jerk. There is satellite television, heating and air conditioning, a firepit for grilling marshmallows, and a propane grill on the porch." She flipped her head around to Kelsey. "Have you spent the night in a cabin outside of Wil's?"

"Never. This has been quite an experience, especially the outhouse for a bathroom."

Bailey and Laney both laughed. Bailey spoke. "You haven't replaced that?"

"No," Wil said. "I'm working on the roof and almost have that completed. The outhouse is next on my list."

"You've been working on that roof for two years," Laney said. "What is taking you so long?"

"I work on it when I have the chance, and I can blame Amanda for the slowness of the project because of all the times she calls me."

Kelsey eyed him. "Wow, blaming your inefficiency on someone who's not even here to defend themselves."

Even Wil joined everyone else laughing at the comment. "I plan on finishing the roof before winter sets in."

"You said that last year, good friend," Laney said.

Wil grinned. "Why are you talking about a cabin when we're sleeping in a tent on the campground?"

Kelsey shifted her head towards Wil. "A tent? You never said anything about a tent."

Wil rolled his eyes. "You never asked. Why do you think we brought them?"

Kelsey shrugged. "I thought they were part of the camping experience."

"They are," Bailey said. "The outdoor camping experience."

Wil took Kelsey's hand. "You'll have a good time."

Kelsey rolled her eyes. "I take it there won't be any

tent service."

Bailey found the perfect spot to camp, and they all climbed out.

Kelsey surveyed the area. "The one thing I'll say about the Black Hills is the beauty everywhere with the trees, hills, and streams." She took off her sandals and dipped her feet into the creek. "It's refreshing."

Wil hoisted a tent onto his shoulders and found a spot to put it up. Kelsey quickly put on her sandals and joined him to help put the tent up. Wil explained what needed to happen. She helped him roll out the tent, inserted the poles through the frame, and raised the tent. He hammered all the stakes in, and it was ready to go. "Good job," Wil said.

Kelsey snickered. "I've never put up a tent before, but it was kind of cool."

Bailey popped up his head. "Why don't the two of you walk over to the Mt. Meadow Store and grab something for supper?"

"Can do," Wil said.

Kelsey grabbed Wil's hand as they walked toward the store. Wil turned toward her. "You're being a good sport with all of this. I know this is something you wouldn't have ever done in your world."

"You're right, but this is enjoyable, partly because of the beauty here, but more importantly because we're doing it together and with your friends."

"They enjoy you also."

"I'm glad because I was worried they wouldn't like me because of my background."

"Don't think like that. And it's not because you're with me; it's because they enjoy being around you."

The two arrived at the store and walked in. Wil

grabbed some logs for the firepit, while Kelsey scoured the shelves for hot dogs and hamburgers and buns, along with chips, and a twelve-pack of beer. "No wine?" she asked the guy behind the counter.

"Sure, we have a red wine sampler and wine beer."

"Sorry, I see it now." She grabbed the wine sampler and waited for Wil to come back in. "I think I have everything we need."

Wil grabbed some marshmallows and graham crackers. "I assume you've never had smores?"

She shook her head.

"It'll be another South Dakota treat for you tonight."

Chapter 18

The four sat around the campfire enjoying their dinner and sipping cups of wine.

"This wine is actually pretty good," Bailey said.

"Have you never had red wine?" Kelsey asked.

"I'm more of a beer drinker."

"I brought beer also but thought maybe wine would go better with the meal."

Laney grinned. "We can learn a lot from you about proper eating and drinking on a campout."

Kelsey blushed. "I'm still a city girl at heart and don't want to throw away all of my creature comforts at once. It's bad enough I have to take a shower in five minutes or freeze to death, cook on two workable burners, and use an outhouse."

They all looked at Wil.

"What?" he asked.

"The object is to keep Kelsey here, so don't you scare her away." Bailey smirked.

Kelsey waved a dismissive hand. "I'm okay with it

all because it takes me out of my comfort zone. I do love everything about Wil's cabin, even the outhouse."

"You'd be the first," Laney said.

Everyone laughed.

The sun had gone down when Bailey and Laney climbed into their sleeping bags. Wil and Kelsey lingered around the campfire.

"How long are we going to stay out here?" Kelsey asked.

"Until it's out or almost out. While lightning strikes are the major reasons for fires, man-made fires can be a nuisance also. Besides, it's awfully peaceful out here at night."

"Have you always wanted to be a mountain man?"

"What?" Wil laughed.

She moved closer to him. "You're like those guys I read about who would rather sleep outdoors than in a nice, comfortable bed with luxurious service." She grinned.

"I do like a nice, hot shower, a hot tub, and a massage once in a while." He chuckled.

"I'll remember that."

Wil pulled her near him and wrapped his arm around her shoulders. "What are you doing out here with me sitting around a fireplace?"

She took a deep breath. "Guess I'm trying to figure out if this is the life I want to live. I like the Black Hills, but I do miss the comforts of a hot bath every night, nice clothes, and being catered to, to name a few things." She finished her wine. "The most important thing is how I feel about you, and I do care immensely for you. I probably even am in love with you, and that scares me. So, I'm weighing my love for you versus a life of ease."

He sighed. "It's hard for me to compete with that."

Kelsey yawned and stretched her arms. "I'm tired, so I think I'll be going to bed."

"I'm going to stay out here for a few more minutes to make sure the fire is completely out."

"Okay. Guess I can figure out how to wiggle into a sleeping bag." She stood up and touched his arm. "Wil, you're making me change how I feel about everything, and that is also scary for me."

An hour later Wil unzipped the tent, crawled in, and zipped it back up. Once he was in his sleeping bag, he turned to Kelsey's voice. "I'm sorry if I hurt your feelings because of what I said. The most important thing to me is not to hurt you because I have strong feelings for you, but this is something I have to work through. Please just give me some time."

"Take all the time you need. I'm in for the long haul. You're the best thing that has ever happened to me."

~

The next morning, Wil was up early firing up the firepit to make coffee and start the eggs and bacon.

Laney joined him a few moments later. "Good morning," she said, wiping the sleep out of her eyes.

"Good morning, sunshine. Did you and your future hubby have a wonderful evening?"

"A gal never kisses and tells." Laney grinned.

Wil grinned right back. "That means nothing happened last night."

"Bailey wishes. What about you two?"

"Nowhere close, which is okay with me."

Laney eyed him, her head tilted. "That's not like

you because you love Kelsey."

"I do, but she's trying to figure out where I stand in her life. Remember she's from a rich family, and I live in a broken-down cabin, so that's a deal breaker right there."

"It doesn't seem to bother her."

"For now. But what about three months from now, next year, or even five years from now? And then there's me chasing after treasures, something I've always dreamed about."

"You really love her?"

"I do, but it probably won't work out because of our different backgrounds."

They both turned at the sound of a tent being unzipped. Kelsey stepped out. "Wow, it was cold last night, but I snuggled in."

Laney grinned. "Why didn't you climb into the sleeping bag with Wil? He would have kept you warm."

Kelsey looked over at Wil and sighed. "I couldn't do that to Wil. Not yet, at least."
She ran her hands through her hair. "What's for breakfast?"

"Eggs and bacon," Wil said.

"Is there anything I can do to help?"

Wil's expression didn't change. "Just think of this meal as me catering to your every whim." He turned over the bacon.

Laney stood and gestured toward Kelsey. "We need to get some more firewood. You can help me with that."

"Great, let me get dressed, and I'll be right out."

Once Kelsey slipped back into the tent, Laney slapped Wil on the arm.

"Ouch," he said. "What was that for?"

"For being such a jerk. She's trying her hardest to meet you halfway and you say something stupid like that? You're going to be the reason she leaves you because of your crappy attitude toward her." Laney smacked him once more.

~

"I can tell Wil's not too happy with me," Kelsey said.

"Wil can be a jerk sometimes."

"No, I deal with jerks all the time, and he is not a jerk. I know I'm in love with Wil, but I'm scared I won't be able to handle any of this because of my background. He'll expect something from me that I won't be able to give him."

"What do you expect he wants from you?"

"That's just it. I'm not sure, but last night I could tell he was hurt when I told him he was making me change how I feel about everything."

"I'm sure it's hard, but also realize it's hard for Wil. He loves you more than anyone in his life. You need to sit down with him and find out where there's common ground between you two. That will mean you'll have to give up some of your luxuries, but so will he have to give up some of the things he enjoys."

Kelsey rolled her eyes. "I'm adamant about a decent toilet."

Laney laughed. "I agree with you there, but please try to understand where he's coming from also."

Kelsey leaned over and picked up a piece of wood. "Is he having a hard time because there is someone else in his life?"

"He probably told you about Lydia."

Kelsey nodded.

"She was important to him, and he hasn't been the same since she died. None of us have seen a glow in him or the spring in his step until you showed up. We all know he cares about you deeply, but he's also aware of where you come from and feels he won't be able to fill all your needs because of all the money you have."

Kelsey picked up another log. "I don't care about all the money. I care about a guy who has my heart, and he's the one."

"If that's how you truly feel, you have your answer. None of this will mean anything if the man you love doesn't have your heart."

"Does Bailey have your heart?"

"He does." She stood. "We had better get back with the firewood."

Kelsey stared toward the campsite. "Today should be an interesting day."

Chapter 19

After breakfast the four went on a hike on the Deerfield Lake trails. They started on Gillette Prairie Road, connected to Deerfield Road, and then headed to Whitetail Loop, which took them around the lake. Then they took a trail up into some rocks where they could look down around the area.

Wil climbed on a boulder, took Kelsey's hand, and pulled her up so hard she fell into his lap. Without a word, she crawled onto the rock and sat down next to him. Bailey and Laney sat on a rock next to them.

"This is so beautiful," Kelsey said. "I've seen some nice spots in the Chicago area but nothing that compares to this."

Laney agreed. "Wil has probably been along every trail in the Black Hills National Forest system. Wil, how does this compare to others?"

Wil thought about it. "There are a lot of unique sites along the George S. Mickelson trail. That one is almost one-hundred-ten miles long, has fifteen trailheads, passes through spruce and ponderosa pine forests, and contains more than one hundred converted railroad bridges and four rock tunnels."

"Wow, that's amazing you have all that information in your head," Kelsey said.

"It is," Bailey agreed.

"That isn't what I meant," Kelsey said. "It is cool that Wil knows all this stuff."

Wil grinned. "It's what I enjoy." He jumped off the rock. "Let's go eat." He helped Kelsey down, and the four followed the trail toward the Gold Run Cafe and Country Store. It was twelve-thirty when they arrived at the cafe. They found a table and looked at the menu. All four ordered a sandwich with a drink.

Laney glanced at her fiancé. "What's on tap for the afternoon?"

"I was thinking about paddleboats or canoes."

"Paddleboats," Laney said.

Kelsey turned to Wil. "Would you go canoeing with me? I've never been on one."

"Sure, we can do that. Did you bring a swimsuit?"

She grinned. "Silly boy, I'm always prepared for everything."

"I should have known."

Their meals came a few minutes later. Kelsey picked up her grilled chicken sandwich and took a bite. "Wow, this is good. Can I have a bite of your chicken bacon Swiss?"

Wil handed her half of his sandwich, and she bit into it.

"This is good also. I'll give you half of my sandwich for half of yours."

"It's a deal."

Once they finished eating, they went back to their tents and changed into swimsuits. Wil had started to come into the tent when Kelsey was donning her swimsuit. She covered her body up. "I'm sorry," Wil said. "I should have knocked or something."

Kelsey smiled at him. "It's okay, Wil. Please, don't be so timid around me. I'll not bite you or yell at you."

"I suggest wearing shorts and a t-shirt over the swimsuit."

She looked confused.

He grinned. "It'll be hard using the oars in the canoe if I'm always looking at you."

Kelsey blushed. "Good thinking." She reached over and touched his hand. "Please, it's not that hard for the two of us to work something out."

A frown covered his face, then he stepped back out of the tent.

When the four were ready, they started walking toward the lake then stopped at a kiosk that rented boating equipment. Wil and Kelsey rented a canoe and pushed it into the water.

"Shouldn't we wait for an hour before getting into the canoe?" Kelsey asked.

Wil helped Kelsey into the canoe. "There is no scientific evidence that swimming after eating is dangerous or increases the risk of drowning. We have waited about forty-five minutes, so we should be okay if you're concerned."

She smiled. "I wasn't concerned. I just wanted to hear you provide more scientific information."

Wil rolled his eyes. "Very funny."

"You sure are grumpy today."

He didn't say anything but handed her a canoe

paddle. "Have you ever paddled a canoe?"

"I have. I remember gripping the paddle with one hand on top and the other a few feet down, reaching forward then pulling the paddle back towards me."

"Good job. Are you ready?"

"Let's do it."

The two paddled for about fifteen minutes and then stopped rowing. Kelsey peered over at Wil. "Are you ever going to forgive me for what I said last night? I was just explaining to you how I was feeling."

"It's not that."

"Then what is it?"

"I'm sorry about the sarcastic remark I made about just thinking of this meal as me catering to you. I should have never said that."

"It hurt, but we're trying to find out how a relationship between the two of us can work. And I want it to work with all my heart."

Wil looked at the sky. "We should start paddling back."

Kelsey grabbed his hands. "Please, Wil, talk to me."

He peered up at her. "I can't right now. Please, be patient with me."

She picked up her paddle and stuck it into the water. Just like that it slipped out of her hand. "Oops," she said.

Wil tried to reach for the paddle, tipped the canoe over, and they both fell into the lake. Wil grabbed for the canoe and reached for Kelsey. "Are you okay?"

"I'm okay. Are you?"

"Yeah, can you help me tip the canoe back over?"

She nodded. The two struggled but finally flipped

it upright. Wil climbed in, reached out his hand, and pulled Kelsey up. She fell into his lap and peered up at him. "Wil, if you want to kiss me, all you have to do is do it."

"What?"

"Twice today, I've fallen into your lap, and we both know you want to kiss me, but you won't."

"Let's head back to the shore."

She grabbed her paddle, and they started again. They returned to the riverbank in ten minutes. Bailey and Laney were waiting for them.

Bailey grinned. "Did you two have fun out there?"

"It was a joy," Wil said.

Kelsey smiled. "I had fun."

After supper the group sat around the campfire chatting and drinking beers.

"I have a question for all of you," Laney said. "What is the one thing you regret in your life?"

Laney ran her hands through her hair. "I'll start. I regret the opportunity I had to visit Paris in high school. My French class was going to Paris for spring break, but I couldn't make it because my parents couldn't raise enough money. The funny thing is the next month they took a trip to Paris themselves."

"That's so sad," Kelsey said.

"What about you, Bailey?" Laney asked.

"Simple, I didn't take the job in California. I wanted so badly to get out of this cold climate and somewhere warm."

"When were you going to do that?" Laney asked.

"After high school I had a job offer at one of the amusement parks but decided against it because I wanted to get my degree, so I stayed here."

"I'm glad you did," Laney said, reaching over and kissing him. "However, once we're married, we can look into it once more."

Bailey stared at her. "You would go?"

"In a heartbeat. I agree with you that it gets cold here. What about you, Kelsey?"

"Wow, that's tough because they're so many regrets. I have all the money I could ever want, but I'm afraid to take a risk."

"What do you mean?" Bailey asked.

"I've been out here for almost two weeks, and I love everything about it, but my life is back in Chicago, and that's all I know. Guess I realize that someday this will all end."

"It doesn't have to," Wil said.

Laney peered at Wil. "What about you?"

"I regret that I can never be with the one I truly love."

Bailey jumped in. "It's a tragedy that Lydia died."

Laney gently slapped him.

"What?" he asked.

She nodded at Wil who was looking at Kelsey.

"Oh."

They chatted for another couple of hours before everyone turned in. Wil and Kelsey climbed into their tent and into their sleeping bags. Wil started to roll over.

"Wil, can we talk?"

He rolled back and gazed at Kelsey but didn't say anything.

She laid her head in her hand and took a deep breath. "All of this is hard for both of us. but please listen to me. I'm an intelligent and sophisticated gal who has operated a multi-million-dollar clothing business for six years, and it's what I enjoy doing, but I also realize you have an adventurous spirit and have your own dreams. I want you to be able to follow your dreams, and I'll be supportive of what you want to accomplish in your life, just as I hope you're supportive of my career and what I want to accomplish in life." She waited for him to say something. When he didn't, she continued. "And that's our biggest problem—that neither one of us has talked to the other about what we want in order to make this relationship work, and believe me, Wil, you're the one I want to spend my life with."

Wil took a deep breath. "You're right when you say we haven't talked about any of what is important to us. We both know when I said my biggest regret was not being with the one I truly love, I was talking about you. I can't compete in your world because you can have anything you want, but all I can offer is a rundown cabin."

"I love that cabin, but I would ask that you please install a regular toilet instead of an outhouse. You think because I have all this money you won't have anything you can give me. That's far from the truth. This weekend we've spent time together, and I've enjoyed every moment of it—grilling, lying in this sleeping bag, following a trail, and even falling into the lake. I enjoyed it because it was with you. You must know I would have never done any of this with anyone else."

She gently reached over and touched his face. "You're right, I'm rich and can have any guy I want, but twice today I fell into your arms by mistake, and both times I was hoping you would take me in your arms and kiss me. That's all I wanted—for you to kiss me. Still, I won't force the issue with you because you're in my heart. We can make it work if we find ways to compromise our lifestyles." She reached over and touched his cheek. "One last thing. You *can* be with the one you truly love because I feel the same way about you."

Wil spoke softly. "You said you were cold last night, so why don't you join me in my sleeping bag?"

She unzipped hers and climbed out, rubbing her hands over cold arms. He unzipped his, took her hand, and pulled her next to him. She eyed him. "Are you sure this is what you want?"

"It's a good start."

"I know—" Before she could finish what, she was about to say, Wil kissed her gently on the lips.

"That's a perfect start."

Chapter 20

The next morning the group disassembled their tents, cleaned up the area, and packed their gear into the vehicle.

"This is the best weekend trip I've ever had," Kelsey said, when they headed down the road toward Nemo. "Thank you all for letting me join you."

Laney turned and smiled at Kelsey. "Hopefully, we can do more of this together. Next time we'll ask Caleb and Amanda to join us."

Wil spoke up, "In another week you two will be married. Are you ready for all of that?"

"I am, but we do have some bad news."

"What's that?" Kelsey asked.

Bailey took a deep breath. "We decided to move to California after the wedding. Yesterday I received a text about a job I had an interest in with a national-forest service near Los Angeles. I got the job, and we're moving there. I start after Labor Day."

"Good for you two," Wil said.

Laney sighed. "Are you sure you're going to be okay, Wil?"

"What is that supposed to mean?" Wil asked.

"It's just that you're connecting with a beautiful gal now, and you always needed someone to talk to when you couldn't figure things out, and it's always been me."

"I can always call you on the phone if I screw it up too bad."

Laney laughed. "That you can. I will miss you, Wil, and I hope the two of you come and visit us whenever you can."

Kelsey jumped in. "I promise that I'll make sure Wil leaves his tiny cabin in the Black Hills to visit his friends."

"That is, if we're still together?" Wil said.

Kelsey took his hand. "I'll make sure we're together."

Bailey and Laney dropped the two off in Nemo just before lunchtime. Once they'd unloaded their equipment, Wil sat outside on the porch.

Kelsey joined him. "Is everything okay with you?"

"I'm not sure. I have so many things running through my mind about the two of us."

"It wouldn't hurt for the two of us to talk about whatever's on your mind."

Wil sighed. "It's hard to imagine that someone as beautiful as you who has as much money as you do, and has the world at her fingertips would even consider being in my life."

"Why? Because you live in a cabin, or because you don't have a million-dollar job? Why should it matter?"

He looked at her. "That's just it. Will it be enough

for you to be in this kind of relationship? A relationship you've said you're not accustomed to."

Kelsey slid over next to him and took his hands. "I've been here two weeks, and not once have I been disappointed about anything we've done. I enjoy the sunsets, I love this little cabin of yours, and I truly love being with you in whatever we do. The only way I leave this place is if you tell me to."

"What about when I start traveling around the world searching for artifact items and treasures?"

"What about when I have to travel for my job? Are you going to ask me to quit or not travel?"

"Of course not," Wil said.

"I would do the same thing for you. We come from two different worlds, and we'll have to compromise on certain things. Our jobs will be one of them. I will miss you incredibly, but I also know you're doing something that warms your heart, and that's important to me." She stood up. "Are you thirsty?"

He nodded.

"I'll be right back." Kelsey came out with two glasses of lemonade.

Wil eyed her. "No beer or wine?"

She shook her head. "I'm trying to wean myself off those two items."

"Is everything okay?"

She sipped her iced tea. "Yes, but drinking less alcohol is one of the things I'm trying to deal with."

"I don't understand."

She took a deep breath and peered into his eyes. "Someday, but not right now, I hope to have children with you, and I don't want to have to worry about that part of my life. It's important to me."

"I've never thought about children in my life."

"I'm sorry if I brought up a tough subject for you."

"It's not that. It's just I never thought about it at this point in my life. I do want to have children someday, but I always thought it would never happen because I'd never find the right gal."

"I never thought about children either until I found the right guy, and my heart has told me I've found him. I'll never pressure you to get married or have children, but someday it will happen."

Wil took a long drink from his iced tea. "I've been thinking about the cabin. If you truly want to stay here with me, I'll take care of the bathroom situation. I've been meaning to do it, but it's never been an issue until you showed up." He smiled. "Consider it taken care of this week."

"Thank you. We can deal with our differences if we talk about them like adults. Please always talk to me no matter what the situation is. I may feel hurt, but it'll never change how I feel deep down about you." She patted her stomach. "I'm hungry."

Wil jumped up. "How about grilled cheese sandwiches?"

~

Monday afternoon, Wil was traveling to the western part of the Black Hills National Forest when his cell phone vibrated. He pulled over to the side of the road to answer it.

"Wil, this is Boris Loe. I heard about your heroic efforts during the large fire in the Black Hills. I hope everything is okay."

"It is, but how would you have heard about it?"

"When I'm interested in someone or something, I

always keep my ear to the ground. The reason I called is I would like you and Kelsey Lawrence to fly to Chicago over the Labor Day weekend to talk to me about Treasure Paradise. I will have plane tickets and rooms available for the two of you, will give you a tour of our facility, and plan a couple of socials to meet some of the people I deal with. I should also tell you upfront Kelsey's parents, uncle, and siblings will be part of the weekend."

"You are serious about this?"

"I am. In fact, our first project is happening right now in Yosemite National Park in California, or I should say we're applying for all the permits and paperwork to find a treasure that was stolen back in the 1800s. There is also some talk that a Bigfoot skull is in the same area, and if it's true, it will be quite a find."

"Let me talk to Kelsey, and I'll get back to you in a couple of days."

"Perfect. One other thing. You may be receiving a call from the national forest supervisor, Carlton Hampton. I think that's his name."

"I work with him."

"Right, but a heads-up. He's good friends with Ben Lawrence. The two of them went to school together at the University of Illinois, and there is speculation Lawrence is trying to get you involved with their treasure hunting group. I just wanted you to be forewarned. If you should decide to join the Lawrence group, I have no issues with that. I just ask that you allow me to pitch what I have to offer also."

"That's fair. I'll call you before Wednesday."

Chapter 21

Kelsey was finishing dinner when Wil walked through the cabin door. "It smells good. What is it?"

"Chicken stir fry with broccoli, red bell peppers, yellow bell peppers, and baby carrots. It's the first time I've made anything like this."

"I can't wait to try it."

"If you want to change your clothes, it'll be ready in a few minutes."

When Wil came back out of his bedroom five minutes later, she turned to him and smiled. "Just in time." Kelsey dished out a plate for each of them. She had already poured them some iced tea. The two carried their plates outside to the porch.

Kelsey eyed Wil. "Well?"

He took a bite. "It's very good. What made you decide to make this?"

She grinned. "I'm enjoying being a domestic girlfriend, or whatever I am at this point. I want to expand my horizons in all facets of my life."

"Let's stick with you being my girlfriend for right now."

"Agreed."

The two were quiet as they ate their dinner until Wil put his fork down. "A guy will be over tomorrow morning to look at our outhouse and figure out how to install a bathroom. I hope you'll be here to assist him with what you want."

"I will and thank you."

"You're welcome. I should ask—don't you get bored sitting out here by yourself?"

She swallowed a bite. "No, I don't. I have been doing my work and have spent time staring out into the wilds, thinking about the cabin. A lot of ideas are running through my mind that I wanted to talk to you about."

"Go ahead."

"You've taken care of the bathroom issue, but what about the roof?"

"The same guy will check the roof also. In fact, he'll look into other options for the cabin that we may have. I had always thought about adding another room but will hold off on that for now. There is one issue about your office, though."

"What do you mean?"

He hesitated. "That extra bedroom could be used for an office."

Kelsey had a smirk. "Are you asking me not only to move in with you but to also move into your bedroom with you?"

"Yeah, right. It may be too soon."

She reached over and kissed him. "No, it's not too

soon. I've been trying to figure out a way to gently talk to you about sleeping together, but you've taken care of it."

"This is awfully awkward."

"Why is it awkward? It's not uncommon for a guy and a gal to make love before they're married. Or don't you want to make love with me?" She grinned seeing him squirm. "It's okay. I'll not pressure you into anything you don't want to do, and I'll stay in the other bedroom and make do with the kitchen table for an office."

Wil took another forkful of broccoli. "Boris Loe called me today and wants us to join him in Chicago over the Labor Day weekend."

"This weekend?"

Wil nodded as he wiped his mouth.

"How do you feel about it?"

"I just told him I'd talk to you and get back to him. He told me your father and uncle are pushing Hampton, the forest-service boss, to talk to me about their little group. Your uncle and Hampton are good friends and went to school together. What are your thoughts?"

"My family only cares about money and more money, so if they're involved it's because they can fill their coffers. My gut reaction is to stay away from them."

"The problem is if I don't work with your family, I'll lose my job in the national forest system here because of the relationship between Hampton and your uncle."

"Would he actually fire you?"

"It wouldn't surprise me." He sat back.

"That's really too bad, but you're right. Businesses

do that all the time."

Wil finished his iced tea. "I plan on letting Mr. Loe know we'll be out there to visit him over the weekend and your family, if you're okay with that."

She took his hand and grinned. "My boyfriend will be meeting the family."

~

It was seven-thirty on Friday when the flight landed at O'Hare International Airport in Chicago. Wil and Kelsey headed toward the baggage area to grab their gear. A guy with a sign was waiting for them as they exited the escalator to the ground level.

"Mr. Bolton and Ms. Lawrence?"

"That's us," Wil said.

"Wonderful. Mr. Loe sends his regrets that he couldn't make it to pick you up because of a last-second meeting."

"No problems," Wil said.

"I'm going to take you to the Ritz-Carlton along the lake. Then I will pick you up at nine tomorrow morning and take you to the Loe Enterprises offices."

"Thank you," Wil said.

Once at the hotel, Kelsey changed into a nice green, strapless dress with matching two-inch heels.

"You always look so gorgeous," Wil said.

She blushed and took his arm as they strolled down to the restaurant. "This is so cool being with you here in Chicago. It's something I've wanted to do with you."

"You're such a romantic."

She reached up and kissed him on the cheek. "With you, that's for sure."

After supper, they sat on lounge chairs on a veranda overlooking the city. "We have a nice view of the lake," Kelsey said. She reached over and took Wil's hand. "The Lawrence family will do everything they can to make sure they control this Treasure Paradise."

Wil was quiet for a moment. "Do you think that's why Mr. Loe became involved? To take them out of the equation?"

"That's a possibility."

The next morning Wil and Kelsey were waiting in the lobby when the driver arrived promptly at nine to take them to Loe Enterprises headquarters in downtown Chicago. Twenty minutes later he pulled into an underground parking lot along Lake Michigan and took them upstairs to the fifteenth floor. Once off the elevator, they entered an open area with a large administrative desk.

The young gal at the desk smiled at them as they walked in. "Mr. Loe and his associates are waiting for you in the conference room. It's this way."

Several moments later the lady opened the door and ushered them into a rectangular room dwarfed by a large table with at least twenty chairs and a large video screen mounted on the east wall. On the south wall a window overlooked Lake Michigan.

"Wil, Kelsey, thank you for joining us," Boris Loe said, shaking their hands. He introduced them to the other eleven people in the room. "These are members of our board of directors. Please join us."

Wil and Kelsey grabbed two seats, and the young lady brought each of them glasses of water along with a bowl of fruit.

"I hoped you enjoyed your hotel rooms," Mr. Loe said.

"It was very comfortable," Wil said. "Thank you

for inviting us to visit your company headquarters."

"I'm glad you could make it. We also plan on visiting our gallery on the tenth and eleventh floor. We own this whole building and have other businesses involved that include finance and archaeology, which is why you're here." He sipped on his water. "I'll provide you with an overview of what we're interested in you doing. For now, the items we've been able to acquire have been easy to procure, but moving forward we're looking at finding more difficult items. That would mean working with archaeologists, governments, and others to find what we're looking for. You're adept at finding the means to get where you want to go, as was evident by saving those three hikers' lives in the Black Hills. You're exactly who we need to find the next of our items."

Wil eyeballed him. "What you're suggesting, Mr. Loe, is that I join a team that goes into countries that most people, including Americans, aren't allowed entry to."

"Not always but yes, there is that possibility."

"You realize I know nothing about treasure hunting or finding artifacts."

"Correct, but you will have the people with you who will help. I have no doubt you'll catch on quickly on what needs to be done."

Wil chewed on a pear. "What about Dr. Regret? This is something he's been researching for many years, and you're just going to take it away from him?"

"I don't do business that way. Dr. Regret will be joining us later today to talk about Treasure Paradise. I know he's having problems funding his projects, and I hope to persuade him to turn the rights over to my company, for which he will be paid handsomely for them."

Wil's head shot toward Kelsey. She grabbed his hand telling him it would be okay. He turned back to Loe. "Mr. Loe, I'd really prefer talking to Dr. Regret about this before I commit to anything. You had mentioned providing funding for his project, but now you're changing your mind. And didn't you say he had already turned the rights over to you?"

"No, Wil, I'm not changing my mind; I'm making sure Dr. Regret is compensated fairly for what he's accomplished. You and I know he can't pull this off without issues, especially from others who are interested in taking over the program."

Wil shook his head. "Mr. Loe, to me this seems no different than what the Lawrences were trying to do to Dr. Regret. And I have a hard time with that."

Kelsey squeezed his hand, and he turned to her. She reached over and whispered in his ear. "Take a deep breath and listen to everything before making a decision."

He nodded then turned back to Mr. Loe. "How about we tour your gallery and then wait for Dr. Regret to show up so I can talk to him?"

"Perfect," he said, smiling.

Kelsey inclined her head toward Wil's. "Boris Loe is not Hank Lawrence. He'll make sure Dr. Regret is taken care of." She grabbed Wil's hand as they joined Mr. Loe for a tour of the facility. They started with the large offices inundated with large-screen video capabilities and up-to-date computer systems. Then they took the elevator to another floor.

"This is the gallery," Mr. Loe explained. "Notice

all the different artifacts from various countries."

"You just keep them up here for people to see?" Wil asked.

Mr. Loe nodded. "But we also hold auctions, and those interested in purchasing the items also visit us. We only sell the items to those who are truly interested in educating the world, which means we deal mostly with museums and galleries. Also we have sold several to private people, but the money we derive from them goes into educating those who are interested in the arts."

"Sounds like a great concept," Wil said.

Mr. Loe nodded. "Believe me, Wil, I don't use the gallery for anything other than helping educate the world about these items. My money is made in the financial world, and because I have that money, I can do good things for others, and that is what I want to do."

The group continued touring the gallery. Wil stopped in front of a large artifact. "Isn't that a colossal head from Central America?"

"I'm impressed," Mr. Loe said. "It's part of the Olmec civilization. Most of the heads are in Mexico City in the National Museum of Anthropology. We were able to find this head from a farmer digging along the Mexican Gulf Coast. We purchased it for a fairly high sum, and it's one piece that will never be sold for any amount of money."

Wil studied the head, then said, "I had read somewhere there could be as many as seventeen of these heads that still haven't been found."

Mr. Loe stared at Kelsey. "That's amazing because only experts in the field know that."

They continued touring the gallery. Wil stopped at a familiar relic. "How were you able to get a piece of the Terracotta Army? That's almost impossible."

"It was, but we were able to acquire this figure through a swap for another item."

Wil stared at him.

"It was nothing illegal, I promise you."

After another hour of surveying the gallery, they stepped back to the elevator. Wil shook his head. "That is amazing. You have almost everything there is to have."

"Not true. You've heard of the Viking runestone? Many have been discovered, but there are still several out there, and then there was a Roman Naval battering ram that was found, but there is more out there. And Dr. Regret has talked about Papua New Guinea, and the destruction during World War II. There are plenty of artifacts still out there."

"It seems you've been doing a wonderful job finding all of these items."

"That is true, but the people we've been working with have changed allegiances to people like the Lawrences and other treasure hunters. I do pay well, but I'll never steal from any country. In our latest find, the group I sent out kept some things for themselves and also passed along information to our competitors. That's a big no-no."

"I see," Wil said. "If I do this, and I'm not saying I will, I'll decide how the operation will be run."

Mr. Loe peered at him. "That's why I'm hiring you—to run the operation your way. Let's go get some dinner and mingle with other interested people. Dr. Regret should be here also with his wife and Mr.

Holloman."

Wil and Kelsey stood together watching others talking to each other. They both turned to a man's voice.

"Wil Bolton, I presume."

He turned to Dr. Regret. "Yes, sir. And this is Kelsey—"

"I know Kelsey through her family, and I'm quite surprised she would even be here with you considering you're dealing with Mr. Loe."

"I'm confused."

Dr. Regret frowned. "Her father and uncle have been doing everything they can to undermine this whole project."

"Kelsey has nothing to do with it."

"Are you sure? I'm sorry, it's all so confusing." He frowned and shook his head. "All this is so hard to process, especially since my wife was diagnosed with cancer."

"We're so sorry to hear that," Kelsey said. "Is there anything we can do?"

"That's why we're selling Treasure Paradise to Mr. Loe. It will help with my wife's medical costs."

"What happened to the Lawrences?" Wil asked.

"I don't approve of their underhanded dealings and the fact that they don't seem to care about what's happening to my wife." Dr. Regret sipped his wine. "But I've made a wonderful decision in selling my rights to Mr. Loe. I now have money my wife's treatment and will continue to receive a percentage of income for the finds that are out there."

Later that night Wil sat on a chair in the veranda of their hotel room. Kelsey joined him wearing one of his t-shirts.

"What's rolling through your beautiful mind?" she asked.

"I'm not sure about all of this. Is business always this cutthroat?"

"It is. Everyone wants the money from the treasure and also the glory that comes with the find."

"Is Mr. Loe the same?"

"He's not. You saw his gallery, and if you could see all the artifacts and treasures he's given to museums and galleries, you would understand."

"I would say it may be easier just to go back to South Dakota, but then I probably won't have a job, so what would I do?"

She climbed onto his lap. "I could always support you, and I'd be okay with it."

"Perfect. I'd be one of those deadbeat husbands who seem to congregate toward gals in Lead and Deadwood."

Chapter 22

Wil and Kelsey caught a taxi to the Loe's mansion located along Lake Michigan. Wil climbed out and stared at the building. Kelsey took his hand. "I take it you've never seen anything this luxurious?"

"You'd be right. There are six pillars up front. How many do they need? And is that about a dozen windows just on one side of the building? Imagine what the back looks like?"

"I'm guessing it faces Lake Michigan. Let's go see."

The two met a butler at the door, who escorted them to the backyard. Kelsey was right. The backyard was two hundred yards from Lake Michigan where boats floated by. A yacht sat next to a huge dock.

"What do you think of the boat?" Mr. Loe said, joining the two. "It's my baby."

"Nice one," was all Wil could think of to say.

Mr. Loe laughed. "I'm sure this is too over the top for you, but I'm sure your lovely girlfriend can relate."

"I can," Kelsey agreed.

"Come, and I'll introduce you to people."

Kelsey noticed her mother standing with a guy, not her father. "I'll catch up with you two."

Kelsey hurried over to her mother. "Mom, who do we have here?"

"Kelsey, I had heard you were going to be here. Meet Mr. Johnson. He's a new employee that your father recently hired to handle finances for this exciting treasure-hunting experience."

"What are you talking about?"

The trio turned to another voice.

"The older you get, the more beautiful you become."

Kelsey smiled. "Is that you, Uncle Ben? Oh my gosh, it is. I haven't seen you in five years."

"Four and half to be exact. I never forget a pretty girl, and you may be the prettiest girl I've ever known."

Kelsey rolled her eyes. "You say that to all the women you meet."

He smiled. "A conversation starter."

"What are you doing here?"

"The same as you, I suspect. I see Mr. Hampton coerced Wil Bolton here so we could talk to him."

Kelsey frowned. "Mr. Loe invited him."

"No problem. We'll still convince him to join our group."

Kelsey glared at her uncle. "Now I understand. You and Loe are pitting him against each other. Wil won't fall for it."

"Why do you say that?"

"Because that's not who he is."

"He's here, isn't he?" Uncle Ben said, hurrying

away.

Kelsey turned to her mother after Mr. Johnson left. "What are you doing, Mom? Is this your latest fling?"

"Not yet, but it will be. Now you, young lady, you found quite a catch. How did you reel him in?"

"It's nothing like that at all. We're taking it slow."

Her mother laughed. "My daughter takes it slow with a guy, especially a handsome guy. You've been with him for two weeks now. How many times have you two climbed into the sack?"

"Not one time, but then again, it's none of your business. Wil is not like any guy I've run across, and the only reason he's here is because he wants to chase down artifacts and treasures. I'll support him anyway I can."

"That bodes well for your father."

"Why are Father and Mr. Loe so interested in Wil?"

"The only thing I know is that they have read about his saving those three hikers and the young girl during a recent fire. They believe he has those intangibles that most people don't have. From my own perspective, he is handsome."

"Knock it off, Mom. Go chase down your latest fling." Kelsey stood shaking her head as her mother hurried over to the bar.

"What has you upset?"

Kelsey turned to Wil. "My mother is a treat. I think she's connected with every one of my dad's new employees."

Wil frowned. "That kind of woman?"

Kelsey nodded. "And that's what I'm so afraid of—being like her and my sister."

"Is your sister the blonde-haired girl over there with tons of makeup and a dress where the top part is ready to fall out?"

Kelsey looked over to where he was looking. "That's her."

"She's tried to pick me up twice in the last fifteen minutes."

"And what did you do?"

"Thought about it," he grinned, "but then figured you were much better."

Kelsey took his hand. "Finally, a guy with some common sense."

A waiter stopped by, and the two grabbed a couple of drinks. Kelsey peered up at Wil. "Do you think my sister's top part is appealing?"

He grinned once more. "Are you asking me to compare you two sisters?"

Kelsey laughed.

"It's not fair because I really haven't seen yours yet."

"Wow, that's the first time you've even mentioned them to me. What's gotten into you?"

"I'm not going to answer that."

She whispered in his ear. "Good choice. Here comes my dad."

Her father hugged her then turned to Wil. "You must be Wil Bolton. I'm glad I could meet you. We're having a get-together tomorrow night at our mansion. I hope you can make it."

"We'll be there."

"Kelsey knows the address. It's nice to see you again, Kelsey."

The guy hurried away to talk to others. Wil peered

at Kelsey. "Is he always that much of a jerk?"

Kelsey had just taken a drink and spit it out. "Many people have thought that. but you're the first one who's said it."

"There is just so much politicking it's ridiculous."

"Welcome to the rich world. They're all jockeying for position."

"Mr. Loe has already offered the job to me. He's offering me more than two-hundred grand with full benefits to take the job, and I can stay in South Dakota. In fact, there is an artifact hunt going on next week in California's Yosemite National Park, that he wants me to be part of it."

"Are you going to take it?"

"Mr. Loe asked me to talk to your father and uncle first before I decide, which is interesting."

"That is interesting, but why would you say that?"

"Because if they're both vying for my services, why would Mr. Loe even ask me to consider a competitor? I also talked to Dr. Regret, and he told me that Mr. Loe has been nothing but nice to him and his wife with his whole situation."

"That's why you agreed to join my family tomorrow night?"

"I did."

The next evening Wil and Kelsey entered the Lawrence mansion. Wil turned to Kelsey. "What are those two trying to do—outspend each other? Mr. Loe has six pillars, and your father has eight plus and at least two more windows."

"But my dad doesn't have the Lake Michigan view."

The gal who hit on Wil joined the two. "No wonder

I couldn't tempt him. He's with my gorgeous sister. It's great to see you, little sister."

"And you too, Crystal."

Kelsey turned to Wil. "This is my sister, Crystal. I hear you two have met each other."

Crystal laughed. "Yeah, I flirted with him last night, but he wouldn't have anything to do with me, which is quite unusual." She turned to Wil. "I'll keep trying because my little sister doesn't stay long with guys. She always finds another guy sooner or later. Besides it's only been two weeks, right, Kelsey?"

"That's about right."

"It's by far not her record for holding onto a guy, but it's getting closer every day. Gotta go, I see someone that looks interesting."

Kelsey frowned. "Now you can see why I'm hesitant about a deep relationship. My mom jumps into bed with the help, and my sister chases any guy who breathes. And you haven't even met my brother. But you are about to."

"Kelsey, it's great to see you," he said, hugging his little sister. He turned to Wil. "You must be Kelsey's latest conquest?"

"I wouldn't say that," Wil said. "Your sister is a wonderful gal who's intelligent, sophisticated, and articulate, which is the type of gal I've been looking for. I'm pretty choosy about the gals I date."

The guy who was several inches shorter than Wil stuck out his hand. "Needless to say, I'm Andy, and it's great to have you here joining our treasure-hunting expedition."

"You're involved?" Kelsey asked.

"I am."

"Where did you get the money?"

"Guess you haven't heard that our father has hired me as a general manager of one of his departments. In fact, he has a position ready for you once you sell your company, and you will sooner or later." Andy turned to a voice. "I need to go, but I can't wait to join you out on the expedition next week."

Wil's mouth dropped. "How did you ever turn out sane?"

Kelsey laughed. "That's why I want to stay in South Dakota."

Wil put his arm around her. "And I thought it was because you kind of liked my cabin."

She laughed again. "I adore your cabin, but I'm in love with you."

~

Kelsey opened her eyes and stared up to Wil who sat on the side of the bed and was looking at something on the wall. "Did you even sleep?"

"I couldn't. All I could think of was this job chasing down artifacts. I've always dreamed about this, but now that I have the opportunity I'm uneasy."

Kelsey popped up and held him. "That's not like you to be scared of anything. You've swung from choppers rescuing animals and humans. What brought this up?"

"I keep thinking you will get tired of me not being home, and that'll be it."

"This is who you are, and I would never stop you from being who you want to be."

"Nor would I stop you. Now that I've finally found the gal I can love."

Kelsey wrapped her arms around Wil's neck. "I'll

be there waiting for you always. You're the guy I'm in love with. Nothing will ever pull us apart. Not my father, not my job, and not the fact that you are traveling around the world doing what you love. Don't you dare worry about me."

Wil pulled her near her and gently stroked her hair. "I'll only be gone two or three weeks at a time, I guess."

"I meant it when I said I would do whatever it took to make sure we're together. I'm in love with you, Wilton Edgar Bolton."

Chapter 23

Late Monday morning, Wil and Kelsey boarded a plane heading back to Rapid City. Once the two were seated, Kelsey took his hand and peered up at him. "I'm glad you accepted Mr. Loe's offer and not my father's. What made you decide to do it?"

"Mr. Loe took care of Dr. Regret, and I'm sorry but your family is really out there."

Kelsey laughed. "That's safe to say. What about your job?"

"I'm sure by the time I return, Hampton will have drawn up the necessary papers to fire me. In South Dakota you don't have to show cause to fire an employee. He has been talking about budget cuts. What about you? What are you going to do?"

She squeezed his hand. "Simple, I'm going to fix up the cabin while you're gone this week, prepare for my trip to Brazil, and pray that you come back in one piece from California."

"Over the next two weeks, we'll get a glimpse of what our life is going to be like. Are you worried?"

Kelsey sighed. "I'm only worried about your

safety. The other I'll deal with fine because I know we'll be together soon."

"When is your trip to Brazil?"

"Gemini has it scheduled for the following weekend. I'm not sure if you'll be back by then."

It was midafternoon when they arrived back in Rapid City. They climbed into Wil's pickup and drove toward the cabin in Nemo. Once they entered the cabin, Kelsey grabbed his hand.

"Isn't this wonderful?"

He looked at the bathroom that had been finished while they were gone.

"It's sealed in, and the shower has warm water for longer than five minutes. In fact, I'm going to test it out right now." She smiled at him, then closed the door and climbed into the shower. A few moments later as she was putting a towel around herself, the door opened. "Wil, what are you doing here?"

He took her in his arms and kissed her.

"Wow, what's gotten into you?"

He lifted her up, carried her to the bedroom, and the two spent the next two hours making love. Once finished, Kelsey laid on his chest. "That was wonderful, and I feel so fulfilled. What happened?"

Wil lifted his head. "I enjoy your upper body parts much better than your sister's."

Kelsey laughed and climbed on top of him. "That earned you another round."

Later while Wil was grilling brats, Kelsey finished getting dressed and moved her stuff into Wil's room. She sat on the side of the bed and smiled. Twenty minutes later, she brought out chips, potato salad, pork and beans she had heated, and some iced tea.

"The brats are done." Wil took them off the grill and dropped them onto the buns Kelsey had put on plates. The two sat on the porch bench and looked out at the beautiful sunset.

"What a weekend," Kelsey said. "That's two wonderful weekends in a row. I could really get used to this."

Wil and Kelsey went to bed early. Kelsey slipped into one of Wil's t-shirts and crawled in next to Wil.

"I've been waiting to sleep next to you for two weeks," he whispered.

Kelsey snuggled into Wil. "Today was well worth the wait."

~

When Wil entered the office the next morning, Amanda was sitting at her desk. "Good morning, Wil," she said.

"Same to you."

She pointed toward the boss's office. "He wants to see you."

Wil shrugged.

"He doesn't seem to be a happy camper today."

Wil took a deep breath and walked toward Hampton's office, then knocked on the door jamb. Hampton looked up and waved him in. "Close the door and have a seat."

Wil did as he was asked. Hampton blew out a breath. "It's been a tough morning; really a couple of tough days figuring out what to do with our budget." Wil waited for the bad news. "I've decided that I'm going to have to cut you loose. I'm sorry."

Wil stared at the guy. "Is it because of me not joining Lawrence's group?"

"That had no bearing on my decision. It was a tough decision, but I decided you were the one to cut because of seniority. You'll receive severance pay equivalent to your last six months wages to help you in the interim as you search for a job."

Wil stared at Hampton. "Anything else?"

"No. Just clear out your gear."

Wil opened the door and strode out, resisting the urge to slam it.

"Are you okay?" Amanda asked.

"I'm fine. Hampton just figured I needed to try something different."

"I'm so sorry," she said, jumping up and hugging him. "What are you going to do?"

"I'm going to clean out my desk and go relax in the cabin."

"Why don't you join us for supper tonight?"

"Thanks, but I just want to clear my head. I'll talk to you in a couple of days." An hour later, Wil stopped at the cabin door for a show he hadn't expected. Kelsey, wearing a bandanna, danced to music as she cleaned the cabin. Wil just stood there and watched. Once she figured someone was staring at her, she whipped around and jumped at the sight of him.

"What are you doing home so early?"

Wil took a deep breath. "Just enjoying the view. I'm home early because Hampton told me to find another job."

She hurried over to him and held him tightly. "You figured that. Was it because of my father?"

"Hampton said seniority, but there are several employees who have been there for shorter periods of time than I have. I don't really care at this point. Boris called me and said we fly to California on Sunday and start searching for the treasure on Monday."

"Let's spend the week doing things together."

"What about your business?"

"I'm the boss, and I'm only a phone call away."

Chapter 24

On Wednesday morning, Wil and Kelsey drove to Hot Springs to the Mammoth site.

"Tell me about this place." Kelsey asked as they were driving toward Hot Springs.

"It's an indoor active dig site where you can view Ice-Age fossils. It's pretty cool."

"You've been there before?"

"Once. It was part of a training program for the forest service. We can go on a self-guided tour, and you can enhance your educational experience with a gaming app."

"It sounds like fun. I'm excited."

It was close to eleven when they arrived at the Mammoth site. Kelsey peered up at Wil. "This is amazing. I've never seen anything like it."

Wil took her hand. "It's a museum with an active paleontological-excavation site where research continues. There is also a sinkhole that formed and was filled during the Pleistocene era." Wil stopped for a moment. "There could be more now, but the last I heard, there were the remains of sixty-one mammoths."

They spent most of the day touring the site and trying their luck at searching for fossils. No luck. On their way back to Nemo, Wil received a phone call.

"Tessa, is that really you?"

"It is. How have you been?"

"On our way back from Hot Springs."

"I'm flying into Rapid City on Friday and was hoping we could spend the weekend with you. We'll be flying out on Sunday."

"Is everything okay?"

"I'll tell you about it when I arrive. I'm bringing Maddie and Jonathan with me."

"What about Steven?"

"He's staying with his father. I'll see you in a couple of days."

Wil turned to Kelsey. "That was my sister. They're flying into Rapid City on Friday."

"Is everything okay?"

"I don't think so. That shortens our vacation together."

Kelsey sighed. "It's okay. I look forward to meeting your family. Are they like mine?"

Wil grinned. "Probably not as weird."

~

Wil was sitting on the porch of his cabin on Friday when his sister pulled into the gravel driveway. Once the car stopped, Maddie jumped out and ran over to Wil. "We're here. Where do we sleep? What are we going to do?"

Tessa, who was getting Jonathan out of his car seat, looked up at Maddie and hollered, "Calm down,

Maddie, and give Wil a chance to catch his breath."

Maddie peered at Wil. "Have you caught your breath yet?"

Wil laughed and rubbed the girl's hair. "I have plenty of things planned."

"Where's Kelsey? Mom said you had a girlfriend. Will she be here?"

"She'll be here in a little while. Have you eaten supper yet?"

"No, Mom said you like to grill hamburgers late, so we're going to wait and see if yours are as good as my dad's."

"Got ya."

Tessa finally made it over with Jonathan. "Sorry about that, Wil."

"Don't be. Maddie and I are fine. How are you, Jonathan?"

"Don't know."

Tessa kissed the side of his head. "I told you Maddie would be here with you, and Wil and Kelsey will make sure nothing will happen to either one of you."

Tessa put the little boy down and took his hand. "Please stay with your sister for a moment while I talk to Wil."

Wil and Tessa moved toward the car. "Is everything okay?" he said.

Tessa shook her head. "It's over, and I'm relieved. But I need some time to myself. Would you take care of the kids? Please?"

Wil hugged his older sister. "Don't worry about Maddie and Jonathan. Do what you need to do."

"Thanks, little brother. I've always been able to

count on you." She hurried over to her kids and hugged them. "Be good for your Uncle Wil and Aunt Kelsey."

Once their mother drove away, Maddie turned to Wil. "Is it time to eat yet?"

"We have a couple of hours yet before Kelsey comes home."

"Where is she?"

"She has some business to take care of."

"Then what are we going to do?"

"How about we go on a hike?"

"In my sandals?" Maddie said.

He shrugged. "I'll make sure we don't run into poison ivy or snakes."

"I hope not."

The two kids and he started up a trail into the hills behind the cabin. It took them thirty minutes to reach the top. Once there, Wil set them both on a large group of rocks, and he joined them. "Look around to the west and you can see Wyoming from here. And if you look to the east, you can see the Badlands."

Jonathan pointed toward the Badlands. "Look, Maddie, there's no grass or trees. That's why it's called a bad land."

"It is, Jonathan. The Indians named it Badlands because there was no water or grass, and it gets really hot and really cold," Wil said.

Maddie spoke up. "Wil, Wyoming doesn't look any different than South Dakota."

"Not where we are. That part of Wyoming is still in the Black Hills. On the other side of that is the wide-open plains, which is much different than where we are."

"Thank you, Uncle Wil," Jonathan said.

"You're welcome. How about we head down the hill and start hamburgers and hot dogs? Kelsey should be here anytime." Wil helped the two kids down off the rocks. They grabbed his hands as they hiked down the trail. Minutes later, he stopped them quickly. "Right there is a rattlesnake."

The two watched as the snake lifted its head, its tail rattling. "Will it bite us?" Maddie asked.

"If we'd have walked any closer, it would have. Right now, it's just checking us out, and if we don't move, it'll slip into the rocks to safety."

They stood there and watched as the snake dropped its tail and slid back into the rocks as Wil said it would. "That was cool," Jonathan said. "A snakebite would hurt."

Wil nodded. "Rattlesnakes are poisonous and can be deadly, so it's always good to avoid them."

"We'll remember that," Maddie said.

When they'd almost reached the bottom of the trail, a car pulled in.

"Kelsey's here," Maddie said. "Can we run down to her?"

"Go ahead. Don't trip."

Maddie took off while Jonathan stayed where he was, holding onto Wil's hand.

"Aren't you going with her?"

"I don't want to see another rattlesnake."

Once the two reached the bottom of the hill, Maddie was chatting away at Kelsey. Kelsey smiled at Wil. "Maddie was telling me all about your adventure on the trail. It sounds like they had some fun."

Jonathan nodded. "Uncle Wil saved us."

"Your uncle's good at that. Are you guys ready to

grill some hamburgers and hot dogs?"

Maddie grinned. "I told Uncle Wil we'll find out if he's better than Dad at grilling hamburgers."

"Well let's go see," Kelsey said. "I have some items I'll need your help with, Maddie."

"Okay."

Kelsey walked over and kissed Wil. "How are you doing?"

"Good, and yourself?"

"Busy day, but I'll tell you about it later. Maddie and I are going to mix up a dessert."

Wil turned to Jonathan. "Are you ready to help me grill?"

"Can I?"

"You bet."

Wil fired up the grill, and Jonathan placed the hot dogs and hamburgers on the grill. He handed the young boy a spatula. "Here, let me show you how to turn the hamburgers over." Wil flipped a couple over. "Now you try."

Jonathan flipped one of the hamburgers over. "Good job," Wil said.

Jonathan grinned. "My dad never let me do this. Or go on a hike."

"Maybe your dad doesn't like that sort of thing."

His lip protruded. "Him and Mom are always fighting."

Wil changed the subject. "You have to watch the hamburgers, or they'll burn. Here's how you take care of the hot dogs."

Once Wil was finished, Jonathan tried it. "Hot dogs are easier to turn."

Kelsey and Maddie came out with chips, potato

salad, and a dessert. "Just in time," Wil said.

They gathered around on the picnic table and sat down to eat. They were eating and talking when Jonathan pointed to Box Elder Creek. "Uncle Wil, is that a bear?"

Wil looked that way. "It sure is."

"Should we go inside?" Maddie asked.

"No, we'll be okay. He'll probably grab some water and then dash into the hills. They're just as afraid of us as we are of them."

They watched the bear drink water. He looked up toward them, then dipped back into the water, and then just like that scampered into the hills.

"Wow, that was cool," Jonathan said. "I'm glad it didn't come here."

It was after nine when Kelsey tucked them into her bed while Wil tucked Jonathan into his bed. She came out and sat next to Wil. "That was a lot of fun. Those kids really like you, Uncle Wil."

They turned to Jonathan's voice. "Uncle Wil, Aunt Kelsey, I'm scared. Think I heard a growl."

"You did, big guy," Wil said. "It was a coyote telling everyone goodnight." He hefted the boy into his arms and sat down on the porch.

Kelsey gazed at Wil and whispered. "Let's go to bed because tomorrow is a big day."

Wil stood up and lifted Jonathan up to take him to bed. Once in the cabin, he kissed Kelsey goodnight, and they went their separate ways.

Kelsey crawled into some pajamas and laid down next to Maddie.

"My Mom and Dad are going to get a divorce."

"Maddie, have you been lying in bed thinking

about this all this time?"

"I have Aunt Kelsey. I'm not scared about it I'm just mad about it."

"Why are you mad?"

"My dad likes someone else."

"You don't know that, and you're only ten years old, so you shouldn't even be thinking like that."

Maddie was quiet for a bit. "Do you love Uncle Wil?"

"I'm still trying to figure it out, but the answer is yes, I'm in love with Wil."

"Why do you love Uncle Wil?"

"Simple, he has my heart and I have his heart, which means we're always thinking about each other. I love spending time with him and hopefully someday we'll be married."

Chapter 25

The next day they spent time around the cabin, walking the trails, and searching for other wildlife. Tessa pulled up to the cabin right before lunch. Kelsey and the kids had been down by Box Elder Creek when Tessa pulled in right before lunch.

They dashed toward her after she got out of the car. "Mom, are you okay?" Jonathan asked.

"I am," she said, hugging both of them. She quickly looked over at Wil who had stepped out of the cabin.

Kelsey noticed Tessa was eyeing Wil as if she wanted to talk to him in confidence. "Okay you two, you can tell your mother all about it in a few minutes. Right now, we need to make some lunch." She led them to the cabin.

~

Once the three went inside, Tessa peered up at Wil. "It's over."

He put his arms around her. "I'm so sorry."

She swiped a hand over her eyes. "Thank you for always being here when I've needed you, and especially when the kids have needed you because we weren't being proper adults for our children. That's the hardest part. I'll make sure that changes."

"What happened?" Wil said, taking her hand and walking to the porch. They sat down on the steps.

"I was right. He's been sleeping with a gal for the past three months instead of going to work. I thought it was happening but couldn't prove it, but he finally had the guts to tell me yesterday saying she made him happy and I didn't. In fact, I've never made him happy. That hurt.

"About six months ago, Cliff lost his job, and for the first couple of months went into a depression and pulled away from me and the kids, all but Steven. You know—his son from his first marriage. Anyway, I kept trying to tell him to find a job that he liked, but he just wouldn't until about three months ago when he found a construction job, or so I thought.

"Although there wasn't a construction job; he was spending time with a young lady, probably twenty-three or so. She became pregnant, and he decided to be with her. Anyway, we're both filing for divorce. He doesn't want joint custody of the kids, and I agreed to waive the alimony payments. I just want him out of our lives, out of the kids' lives."

Tessa took another breath. "Yesterday and this morning, I was interviewing for a bank-president job in Deadwood and was offered the job, so I'll start on Monday. I took the job because the kids wanted to be near their uncle." She smiled at Wil. "I see you've met a beauty."

"Yes, I have. I'm just not sure what'll happen. She comes from the rich side of town, and well, look at the cabin."

Tessa took her brother's hand. "Forget about the money because Kelsey appears to be in love with you, not money. I see the glow in her eyes when she's with you, and that's just in the short time I've seen you two together. And Maddie would never allow you to be with a gal she doesn't like. Remember those two girls you were dating? Maddie didn't like them one bit, and she was only six at the time."

They both laughed.

Wil squeezed her shoulders. "I don't believe it'll be that tough for the kids. Jonathan doesn't seem to have a relationship with his father, and Maddie doesn't seem to think much of him."

"She doesn't, and she hasn't for a few months. They both think of you as their father, and I'm glad they have a male role model. Promise me you'll always be there for them?"

"No question I'll be there for them and for you. You're my big sister, and you've always been there for me."

"Thank you. I hate to ask you this, but could you watch them at certain times when I have to travel for work or attend events?"

"Just call when you need me."

"What about your new job?"

"It shouldn't interfere, but if it does, we'll work it out."

Tessa wiped away the moisture from her eyes. "The worst thing about all of this is that I'm not even disappointed or hurt. What does that say about me?"

"You've had a feeling that it was over, so maybe you've already adjusted to it. The kids will be fine."

"I know they will because you are in their lives, and they love you."

"I'm glad you're going to be here because Kelsey is going to need someone for her."

"What do you mean?"

"Tomorrow, I'll be flying to California on my first treasure-hunting expedition."

"That's exciting. Good for you. Of course, I'll be here for you. I'm sure Maddie will make sure she's taken care of."

"She didn't kick Kelsey out of bed last night, so there's hope."

~

On Sunday, Kelsey and Maddie dropped Wil off at the airport. When they reached security, Wil turned to hug them.

"You make sure you call Kelsey when you get to San Francisco," Maddie said.

"Yes, Mom."

Maddie giggled. "She needs to know that you're safe because you can get yourself into trouble at times."

Wil lifted her up and kissed her on the forehead. "She's already figured it out. You take care of her while I'm gone?"

"I promise."

Wil set her down and took Kelsey into his arms. "I'll miss you, pretty girl."

"And I you." He kissed her solidly on the lips.

A few minutes after Wil climbed onto the plane, it took off for San Francisco. He was to meet a man named Ollie Reynolds, whose daughter, Dr. Sarah

Reynolds, was the lead archaeologist on the dig site in Yosemite National Park.

He started reading his information packet once more, remembering some of the details. Dr. Reynolds was a renowned archaeologist from a major California university and had been searching for a treasure that was allegedly stolen in the 1800s.

Also with the group were her assistants, Mitch and Delilah. There was also a guy named Xavier Holloman, who was a bodyguard for Mr. Reynolds, Sarah's father. Britton Kenyon, a park ranger at Yosemite National Park, was also involved.

He landed midafternoon in San Francisco. Once he was on the ground, he quickly texted Kelsey to let her know he had landed safely. She texted immediately that she missed him and loved him.

A young guy, probably in his early twenties, was waiting for Wil once he left the baggage area.

"Hi, Mr. Bolton, I'm Mitch Kirkwood, a research assistant for Dr. Reynolds. She asked me to pick you up and take you to the Reynolds' house."

"Nice to meet you, Mitch," Wil said, proffering his hand.

The two arrived at the Reynolds' house—more like a mansion—an hour later in San Jose. It wasn't quite as large as Kelsey's parents', but it was comparable. The security searched the two of them before they could enter. Once they did, a butler escorted them to the pool area where a group of people were congregated.

"The man with white hair is Dr. Reynolds, and the woman with the long black hair is another of her assistants, Delilah."

The older man greeted them. "I take it, you're Wil

Bolton?"

"Yes, I am, and you must be Mr. Reynolds."

"I am. Boris said you would be easy to deal with, and I see you seem to be a nice guy."

"Thank you."

"Come and join us. The party's starting."

Wil grabbed a glass of wine and stood out of the way watching everyone mingle. Dr. Reynolds joined him with a drink in her hand. "It's nice to meet you, Mr. Bolton."

"You as well, Doctor." "Please call me Sarah. We're going to be working together, so no need to be formal."

That night Wil called Kelsey to see how she was doing.

"Maddie and Jonathan said to tell you hi," Kelsey said.

"How's the sleeping arrangement going?"

"Well, I'm crashing with Maddie, and your sister is in our bedroom. Jonathan is on the couch and loving it. It was cute when he heard the rooster he came running into our bedroom and jumped between Maddie and me. Maddie held him and comforted him until he fell asleep."

"I'm glad it's working out. Any timetable on a place to live for Tessa?"

"She's hoping by the end of the week. She's received at least three calls from her husband today, and each time she became more stressed. Is he a jerk?"

"I didn't think he was, but Tessa never talked about things like that."

Kelsey laughed. "Just like her brother."

"I'm trying to do better. Are you okay with this?"

"Of course, I am. I love you, Wil, and these two kids are a barrel of laughs. They do love their uncle. Maddie has told me at least five times today what's expected of me, and Jonathan has also told me that Wil is very particular about certain foods. I didn't know you preferred hot dogs over brats."

Wil laughed. "I do."

"I should probably get off the phone because Maddie needs something. I love you, and be careful."

The next day the group headed toward Yosemite National Park and in particular, Chilnualna Falls. When they arrived at the south entrance of the park, Dr. Reynolds led the group to a waterfall where her research had suggested there might be an entrance.

Wil found a way underneath the waterfall, and the others followed. The group consisted of Wil, Dr. Reynolds, Mitch, Delilah, and Holloman, whom Dr. Reynold's father sent as a bodyguard.

"I may have found something," Wil said.

Holloman was right beside him. "What is it?"

"It looks like there's a crack or something right here."

Just like that it started to shake, and the two backed up quickly. The crack opened wide enough for a body to slip through. Wil hurried through, followed by Holloman, and then the rest of the group. It was completely dark inside.

Holloman turned on his headlamp and moved to the front while everyone turned on their helmets' lamps. Wil worked his way through the tight spaces until he reached an open area. Just like that the ground started shaking again, and Mitch, rushed back to Wil.

"We're trapped. The opening has closed."

Chapter 26

On Thursday, Kelsey and her group climbed onto a Learjet flying them to Rio for their weekend meeting with Roberto Santiago. It would be close to a seven-hour flight. Having arrived in Chicago a day earlier, she had to smile thinking of what Maddie had told her before she left.

"We'll watch over the cabin and make sure no bears or mountain lions get through the front door."

Although Kelsey had not heard from Wil for a couple of days, she wasn't too concerned because she knew he'd be in an area where reception would be difficult at times.

The hotel they were staying in was on one of the many beaches in the city. It was close to one, Rio De Janeiro time, when the jet prepared to land in Antonio Carlos Jobim International Airport. They flew over the treasured icon, Christ the Redeemer statue sitting on the top of a mountainside.

"Isn't that beautiful," said Alexis, who along with

J.J., had joined the tour.

Everyone stared at the sight.

Dolby, Gemini's fiancé, explained what he'd learned. "It was constructed between 1922 and 1931, and it stands ninety-eight feet high. Its arms stretch ninety-two feet wide. Interesting that it's made of reinforced concrete and soapstone."

JJ glanced at the guy confused.

Dolby smiled. "I'm a construction engineer in Chicago." He also explained the statue was located at the peak of the twenty-three-hundred-foot Corcovado mountain in the Tijuca National Park overlooking the city. "It's considered a symbol of Christianity around the world and has become a cultural icon for both Rio de Janeiro and the rest of Brazil." He took a breath. "Listen to this, it has been voted one of the new Seven Wonders of the World."

After the jet landed, they walked through the terminal and grabbed their gear. Waiting for them were members of Santiago's team.

A man with a salt-and-pepper mustache stepped forward. "My name is Alberto Sanchez. I hope you enjoyed your flight. I'm going to take you to the Hilton Rio de Janeiro Copacabana."

"Thank you, Mr. Sanchez," Kelsey said.

They climbed into a van that took them toward the hotel, arriving there thirty minutes later. As they got out of the van, Sanchez told them there would be a social event later that night in an upstairs meeting room.

Once inside, a young lady was waiting for them. "My name is Rosalita Ancov. I'm your guide for the weekend."

"Thank you, ma'am," Kelsey said.

"Your rooms are on the third floor, and all face the Atlantic Ocean. A wonderful view. Please follow me."

The group took the elevator to the third floor. Once in her room, Kelsey laid her suitcase on the bed, walked over to the window, and marveled at the breathtaking view. She took a photo from her cell phone and sent it to Wil. *Look what you're missing.*

Kelsey had hopped into the shower when she thought she heard a knock on the door. She quickly grabbed a towel and climbed out, then opened the door a bit.

"Ms. Lawrence, Mr. Santiago is waiting for you in the lounge downstairs," Ms. Ancov said.

"The social doesn't start for another hour."

"Understood, ma'am. He has some important details to talk to you about beforehand."

"I'll be there in fifteen minutes."

Kelsey took her time getting dressed, but didn't put on makeup, not wanting to cater to the man's whims. She didn't trust Santiago yet. He was a womanizer, so she wanted to avoid any chance he thought she wanted him. She took the elevator down to the lounge and found Mr. Santiago sitting talking to another man.

When she walked over, he looked up. "Ms. Lawrence, glad you could join us," Santiago said, rising to his feet and giving her a kiss on the cheek. "Please meet Rafael Condor. Dr. Condor has read about your new business and is interested in talking to you about it."

"Which new business are you talking about, Mr. Santiago?"

Dr. Condor jumped in. "Treasure Paradise. I'm an avid treasure seeker. I didn't mean it like that. I meant to say I'm interested in searching for little-known artifacts and learning more about past civilizations."

"Are you an archaeology professor?"

"Yes, Ms. Lawrence. Ph.D. degree from University of Sao Paulo. The best school in Brazil. One of the best in the world."

Kelsey eyed the gentleman who had to be in his fifties with graying hair, dark eyes, and a clipped beard. Both men wore laid-back dress of clothes that included shorts and sandals.

"May I order you something to drink?"

"I'll have black tea or the proper name here in Brazil, *cha-preto*."

Dr. Condor smiled. "Very well. Please join me here at the table."

Santiago glanced at the two. "I have some last-minute items to prepare before tonight. I'll see you later, Ms. Lawrence."

She nodded at him. Dr. Condor took her hand. "Please join me."

He pulled out a chair and pushed it in for her.

"Thank you," she said. "How kind."

"I've heard you are very kind also."

"Thank you."

"I know this is abrupt for you, and I apologize. Santiago had told me you would be here, so we could talk."

"How does Mr. Santiago know you?"

"His sister is a student at my university. I met him through her. He's very active in the community. Especially with the women."

"Dr. Condor, you'll have to contact my father about the venture. I have nothing to do with it."

~

Wil led the group further into the cave, trying to find another way out. They were rounding a corridor when the earth started shaking once more. He lunged forward and pulled Holloman away from a wall that came crashing down, separating them from Dr. Reynolds and the others.

The two lay there, coughing, and stared at the barricade. Holloman looked toward Wil. "You saved my life. Thank you."

"How are we going to get out of here?"

The two sat there catching their breath before Wil climbed up. "Maybe we can circle around and come back from another angle."

"It's worth a try."

They slowly made their way around the labyrinth, but after fifteen minutes, they couldn't reach back to where they had come from. Wil tried his cell phone. Nothing.

"We might as well rest for the night and continue the search tomorrow," Holloman said. "Have you ever heard of such a thing—two earth trembles in a fifteen-minute period? It's like someone doesn't want us to find what we're looking for."

Wil, who had slid down against the wall, nodded. "I had read that this area of Yosemite had seen people disappear. Some were found, others weren't. There was never an explanation about what happened or if there was, no one ever said anything." Wil pulled out a protein bar out of his backpack and reached out to Holloman. "Would you like one?"

"I'm not hungry, but I did bring something to eat. Thanks anyway. The only good thing I can say about all of this is they do have food and water, so that'll help until we find them."

Wil eyed Holloman. "You're not Dr. Reynolds' bodyguard, are you? You work for Lawrence?"

Holloman took a deep breath. "How did you figure that out?"

"Boris Loe never said anything about a bodyguard being involved in this expedition, and Dr. Reynolds never mentioned you at all."

Holloman chuckled. "You don't realize that Dr. Reynolds and her father also work with Lawrence."

"Wow, this is all messed up. How would Boris Loe not know any of this?"

"He didn't because he hired Dr. Reynolds for this expedition, not knowing that her father and Lawrence had an agreement that if her daughter was ever involved with a find, they would split the royalties. It is all messed up."

Wil chewed on his protein bar. "And you think this is okay?"

Holloman shrugged. "I've seen worse things in the Navy Seals. Many times, we would go after a target, and just like that we'd have to abort the mission because the guy was friendly or the opposite, he turned rogue. Crappy world."

"How long were you in the Navy Seals?"

"Four years, which was way too long. It was hard to erase the images of death we saw. I took this job with Lawrence at the start to protect his daughter, Kelsey. Then she hooked up with Nolan Gant, who was Hank Lawrence's protege. Both are evil men."

Wil sipped on his water. "You were supposed to bring Kelsey back, but you didn't because you had fallen for her?"

Holloman nodded. "She's not only a beautiful gal, but also she's very intelligent. I don't know how she became a Lawrence because she's so different from everyone in her family. As you could see from the one time you met them, they're all fruit loops."

Wil laughed. "That's one way of putting it. Is Kelsey for real?"

"What do you mean?"

"You know she's living with me, correct?"

Holloman nodded. "And that's a good thing because from what I can gather, you're a straight shooter. Lawrence had sent me to retrieve Kelsey and take care of you, but once I saw how happy she was, I couldn't do it."

"That's what the two guys chasing Loe's brother was all about? The sheriff was right when he said Lawrence was involved with it."

Holloman nodded once more. "You don't want to cross that man or those who are running drugs and laundering money in the Black Hills and other places around the world. They'll never get caught because they have so many people in their pockets, and we have no clue who they are."

"Why are you telling me all of this?"

Holloman reached into his pack and pulled out a pint of whiskey. "Because you saved my life, and Kelsey Lawrence thinks a lot about you. The gal is in love with you, and that's a first for her. I've known her since she was a baby and as she grew into a woman, guys flocked to her everywhere she went." He took a sip of his whiskey and offered a shot to Wil, who shook his head. "Kelsey's dated a couple of guys and was engaged to Gant until she ran into you in the Black Hills. She called me that first night and told me she had found the one for her."

"I don't understand your relationship. What you just said indicated you love her."

Holloman took a deep breath. "Because she is my daughter. Her mother and I had an affair when I was in the Navy Seals. I was home on leave and ran into her at a bar in Chicago, where we're both from. She couldn't stand Hank Lawrence even then, and they had just married. She had always loved a garbage collector, but because she was rich, her parents told her it could never happen." He took another sip. "We were both drunk, found a hotel room, and Kelsey was conceived. You're the first to know, and if you say anything—" he grinned.

"You'll have to kill me." Wil chuckled. "Why are you telling me all of this?"

"We're never going to get out of this. And if we do, and Hank Lawrence finds out, there'll be hell to pay."

"Isn't the clothing and design business Kelsey's?"

"It is. She started it from scratch and has done a wonderful job. Her father and uncle tried to steal it from her a couple of times. Enough talk, I'm going to sleep." Holloman curled up next to the wall. He stuck his head up one last time. "Please take care of my little girl and don't think for a moment she doesn't love you."

Chapter 27

Kelsey walked into the social event and looked around, then heard a voice behind her.

"Ms. Lawrence, where's your fiancé?"

Kelsey noticed the man, Santiago, seemed kind of edgy. "It didn't work out."

"Please join me. There are a couple of people I'd like you to meet."

Kelsey made sure Gemini was with Dolby before she walked over with Santiago.

"Mr. Rondo, he's one of the premier bankers in Brazil. This is Ms. Kelsey Lawrence, owner of an international clothing and design company."

"Ma'am, I've heard much about you. Nice to meet you."

Mr. Rondo turned to a younger man. "This is my son, Javier. Twenty-five years old, and an up-and-comer, as you Americans would say."

"Nice to meet you, Mr. Rondo."

"Javier." The young man smiled.

Kelsey didn't respond to the comment. She glanced at the older Rondo. "Is your bank interested in providing funding for Mr. Santiago's clothing enterprise?"

"We've thought about it. A lot depends on what you have to offer. Santiago said he is interested in forming a conglomeration with your clothing and design company."

"We have discussed it. Tomorrow we'll have the opportunity to see the sites. Then we'll have a better idea of how we can work together."

The older Rondo smiled at Kelsey. "I'm sure you'll make my younger son part of this visit."

"That's up to Mr. Santiago. We are guests in your country."

Mr. Rondo turned to Santiago. "What about it, Roberto? Is Javier part of this visitation?"

Santiago smiled. "I'll make sure he's included."

"Wonderful, it's going to be a wonderful evening."

Kelsey spent several hours talking to those at the party. Around nine she called it a night and started out the door.

"Can I escort you to your room?" Javier asked with a smile.

Kelsey returned the smile. "No thank you. I'll be fine."

The young man frowned at Kelsey. She hurried to the elevator and went to her room, immediately falling asleep on the bed. She jumped up at the knock on the door.

Alexis was outside. "Let's go. We're going to some nightclubs. Guests of our host."

Kelsey took a deep breath. "Let me put my shoes

on."

Within half an hour, the group was at one of the many downtown nightclubs in Rio. Kelsey stood at a table with the others. Javier and Santiago joined them with several other men and women. Some dance songs came on.

"Let's go," Alexis said to JJ, who grabbed Kelsey's hand pulling her out on the dance floor. Santiago and Javier joined them. They danced for an hour together. Then a slow song came on. Javier asked Kelsey to dance.

"No sir. My fiancé is the only man I dance slow dances with." She turned and returned to the table. Santiago joined her. "Ms. Lawrence, you were rude to Javier."

Kelsey glared at him. "No, sir, I wasn't. There are times when I draw the line, and dancing a slow dance with a man other than the one I love is on that list. I'm sorry if I offended the man, but it won't happen."

They ended up going to a couple of other clubs before calling it a night.

Kelsey climbed into her bed at midnight, still not having heard from Wil.

~

Wil tried to move his body. He hurt like hell. Again, he tried his radio but heard nothing. Wil finally struggled to his feet. He looked around and found he and Holloman were sealed in. Maybe this was what happened to the others. He reached into his backpack and found a flashlight and shined it around the cavern. There were two tunnels—one going to the north, the other to the south.

Holloman who was beside him, said. "Why don't

you take the north tunnel and I'll take the south tunnel?"

Wil shined the light on the ground to see if he could find some footprints. Luckily, there were two sets of footprints. They could be carrying a third person.

Wil followed the footprints through the tunnel. He had traveled for an hour when he took a break. He sat down and reached into his backpack to grab something to eat. Deep inside he found a protein bar that he brought with him at all times. He ate it and drank some water.

Wil closed his eyes for a minute, the oxygen was low, and he was getting sleepy. When he opened his eyes, he jumped back when he saw dark eyes staring at him. When he did, the wild animal took off running away. He'd never seen anything like that creature before in his life. It looked like some kind of fox. He climbed off the ground and continued down the tunnel.

Wil had traveled a couple of hours when he found a broken shoe. Stowing it in his bag, he continued until he heard a noise. He stopped and listened again. Voices. Wil hurried toward them.

Another hour and he found three people huddled together trying to keep warm.

"Dr. Reynolds, you're still alive."

He bent down on his haunches. "Are you hungry? Thirsty?"

Dr. Reynolds just nodded. The other two were worse off. Wil reached into his pack and pulled out his water canteen. He handed it to her who drank thirstily. She handed the canteen to the other two. Wil pulled out the bars and provided each one of them with a protein bar, then stood. "Sit here and relax. I'll be back with

Holloman." Wil hurried back through the caves and found Holloman about an hour later.

Holloman shook his head. "No luck."

"I found them, and they're still alive."

He, along with Holloman, retraced his steps to Dr. Reynolds and the other two late in the afternoon, as his watch indicated. Wil took a deep breath, trying to take in as much oxygen as he could. "We'll find a way out of here."

"There's no way out of here," Sarah said. "Dead end after dead end. We've tried."

Wil glanced down to the other end of the tunnel. "How far did you get?"

"This was it. No more oxygen in our tank. Dead tired. And hungry."

Wil searched the tunnel. "I'll take a walk up a ways. See if I can find anything. Anything at all."
He bent down once more on his knees. "I promise I'll be back. Can you help them out, Holloman?"

"Yep, find us a way out of here."

Wil scrambled down the tunnel. After he'd gone about three hundred yards, he stopped. He had to double check what he just saw. A chest of some kind. He opened it up. Jewels and a crown. Could this chest be what Sarah Reynolds was looking for?

There were a multitude of bones lying on the cave floor around the chest. He noticed more bones further away. Wil followed the trail of bones for thirty minutes until he reached a dead end. He figured that was what happened to the other trying to find a way out.

A glowing spot along the wall caught his attention. He quickly dived down and dug into the ground. Several minutes later, he stopped and peered at a skull of sorts. It was a large skull. Had he actually found the skull of Bigfoot? Wil picked it up, placed it into the chest, and made his way back to Holloman, Sarah, and her two research assistants. He plopped down next to Sarah.

She peered up at him. "Anything?"

He smiled at her. "You found your pot of gold. In this case, a treasure chest. And a large skull."

Her eyes lit up. "I did?"

"A chest with tons of bones lying around it. These people also found the chest, but died as they were trying to find a way out."

Sarah tried to stand up. "We have to go there. I need to see it."

"No, ma'am. You need rest. Tomorrow we'll go check it out. How are the other two doing?"

"Mitch is really hurting. Delilah is not much better."

Holloman had checked on Mitch. "Looks like he busted a leg. He said it hurt like hell, so I grabbed his leg, talked to him quietly, and I snapped it. He screamed and passed out."

Wil slid over to Delilah whose face was hot to the touch. "Anything else happen?"

"No sir. I feel really sick."

Wil reached into his backpack and pulled out a bottle of aspirin. "This should help some." He gave some tablets to both of them. "The best thing is for you both to get some sleep. Tomorrow we'll figure out a way to get out of here."

Sarah glanced up at him. "It's not looking hopeful. I've done research on this cave for a couple of years and wasn't able to find many exits. It was like the mountain had just opened up when the tremor hit. And then another closed it. Somebody doesn't want us here."

"We'll worry about it tomorrow. Get some sleep."

The three were fast asleep, but Wil and Holloman were wide awake. Holloman looked over at him. "We found what we're looking for."

Wil nodded. "Now the tough part comes. What are you going to do about it?"

Chapter 28

The next day, Kelsey and the others from Chicago started their tour of the Ecomuseum of Santa Cruz. Santiago explained, "the museum's main mission is to preserve the cultural and natural heritage of the neighborhood of this area of Brazil. The museum develops educational, communicational, and documentation activities, as well as its history, its territory, its inhabitants, and its ecosystem."

The next stop was the ethnicities mural. "This is one of the largest graphite angels in the world and is a newer tourist attraction in Rio," Santiago said. "It was inspired by the Olympic rings representing the five continents." Santiago and the group spent the rest of the day touring other sites of Rio. They also spent time touring clothing facilities.

On the bus back to the hotel, Kelsey turned to Santiago. "It seems the marketing angle here revolves around Brazilian art."

He nodded. "Art is very important to our culture."

She thought for a moment. "I'm impressed with the clothing facilities, but I'm also concerned about the pay your employees receive. Are they comparable to those in the states, or are they like the other countries in South America?"

Santiago sighed. "The wage scale is much lower than in America. We're working to increase that. Hopefully if we join your group, that will occur sooner than later."

Mr. Rondo, who had joined them for the tour, leaned forward. "There are significant disparities between the rich and the poor in Rio. Different socioeconomic groups are largely segregated into different neighborhoods."

"That's sad. It sounds like it's no different than parts of Chicago."

"Correct, Ms. Lawrence," Mr. Rondo said. "Large numbers live in slums known as *favelas*. It is estimated that six percent of the population live in these *favelas*."

Santiago added. "Government initiatives have started to deal with the problem. It includes moving people from favelas to housing projects, then improving conditions in the favelas and bringing them up to par with the rest of the city. Rio has more people living in slums than any other city in Brazil according to a 2010 Census."

Mr. Condor broke in. "To offset the negativity you see in the city, Rio de Janeiro continues to be a main cultural hub in Brazil. The architecture embraces churches and buildings dating from the sixteenth to the nineteenth centuries. They are blending history with the progress of the twenty-first century."

After a lull, Santiago jumped in. "Tomorrow, we'll

take you to the Biblioteca Nacional, which is the national library. It has collections of more than nine-million items. The National Museum of Fine Arts and the Natural History Museum are also on the agenda. We'll conclude the day at one of the numerous street parties, known as a *bloco*. A bloco acts as rehearsal for different Samba schools leading up Rio's most annual event, the *Carnival*. It lasts four days and draws almost five million people. The highlight is the center of the city's collection of floats at *sambrodromo*. Hundreds work all year to prepare floats and costumes to earn a place in a special-group category or promotion to the elite group. Everyone enjoys the event."

~

As Wil checked on Mitch, he was relieved to find him sleeping peacefully, and his fever had gone down. Delilah had been sleeping for the past hour. He slid down next to Sarah who was still awake. "They should be okay. It must have been tough dragging Mitch."

Sarah nodded. "Took a lot out of us, but it had to be done."

Wil handed her some water.

"Thanks."

"Explain to me who hid the chest down here."

Sarah finished taking a swallow and handed the canteen back to Wil. "There are a couple of theories. One is that the Knights Templar made it this far with their gold and tried to start over on the West Coast. It's really hard to imagine, but it is possible."

She took a deep breath. "The second theory and probably the most logical is that the treasure was stolen from the Presidio near San Francisco in the 1800s, probably before the California Gold Rush. The thieves were chased into Yosemite. They probably were lost, and those searching for them just gave up."

"What is the significance of the treasure?"

"All those jewels. Most important is a gold crown. Many say it may be worth two to three million dollars easily if not more. The treasure isn't as important to me as what this area signifies."

"What is that?"

"Many people have been lost around here and never found. We could be the next batch of people who've been lost. The tremors caused the entrance at the waterfall to close, but why can't it be found again? And there are many archaeologists and anthropologists who believe that a native group lived in this area to protect themselves from other Native Americans and settlers to this area. So you see, there are lots of questions without any answers. Finding the treasure would solve that portion of the mystery. Once I have a look at those bones, that may provide some more answers."

Wil touched Sarah's hand. "Right now, you need to get some sleep."

She peered deep into his eyes and smiled. "Realize this isn't the time, but when we get out of this, I want to find out more about who you are. Maybe build a relationship. And it's not because you saved my life. There's just something about you that I find interesting."

Wil smiled. "Sarah, you're not yourself. Try to get some sleep."

She smiled back at him and tapped his arm. "No, Wil Bolton. I'm a woman, and there is something about you that draws me to you."

"Dr. Reynolds, you're a wonderful gal, but I already have a woman that I'm totally in love with and hope to spend my life with." Later Wil woke up and peeked over at the others. Sarah was missing. He jumped up and checked on the other two. Their fevers were gone. He hurried over to where Sarah was. She was on her knees looking at the skull.

She squinted up at him and smiled. "Did you sleep well?"

Wil glanced at her. "Yes, I did. I take it you had a good night's sleep and are raring to go."

"I am. And it's even better than I expected."

"What's that?"

"Although some of these bones are from the last few decades, some are from the era in which the treasure was supposedly stolen. Others even earlier."

"I don't understand."

"I'm trying to piece it together. What's also interesting is that a couple of these bones are of some kind of big cat or even a lion. That would be unheard of. Cats don't frequent caves. However, the cat could have landed here like we did. I believe the tremors have everything to do with these bones being here."

"What do you mean?"

"The tremors close the entrances. Why couldn't they open the entrances? Which would mean people searching for treasure or even exploring could have ended up here and never survived."

Wil grimaced. "That doesn't bode well for us."

She smiled at Wil. "We'll just have to wait for the next tremor."

"I'll continue searching for another way out. If a tremor does occur, we'll head to the entrance."

Wil trekked further down the tunnel. He traveled about an hour when he ran into three different tunnels. He took a shallow breath and decided to follow the one to the left. About an hour later, he felt a slight tremor. He glanced up and saw an opening above him to the left. Wil reached quickly into his bag and grabbed some rope he carried with him. He tied a rock around it and threw the rope up toward the hole. It took him four tries before he was able to connect with something solid.

Wil quickly climbed the rope, reached the top, and climbed out. He had no idea where he was. There were some high peaks in the distance. He tied the rope around a large tree and slid back down into the cave, then raced toward Sarah. "Found a way out."

Holloman jumped up and his eyes looked at him. "The tremor?"

Wil nodded. "Let's go."

He grabbed Sarah's hand and pulled her up. She lost her balance and fell against him. They locked eyes for a split second. "We have to move, Sarah."

She nodded and hurried toward the other two. Wil took the skull and placed it into his backpack. If nothing else Sarah would have the crown to prove what she had found. They helped the others to the area where they could climb out.

"How are we going to do this, Wil?" Sarah asked.

"Holloman will go up first, then you and I'll carry Delilah on my back, then come back down and tie Mitch onto it, and so forth. I'll do the same thing for the chest."

"You're going to bring the chest up?"

"I'll try hard."

The first two trips up and down went off without a

hitch. Wil climbed back down to tie Mitch around the waist. He shimmied up the rope, catching himself twice on wedges, but the others were able to pull him out of tight spots and get him up.

Once he was settled, Wil quickly climbed down and hurried toward the chest. He closed it and wrapped it the best he could to keep the skull and jewels from falling out. He flipped it over his shoulder and hustled toward the hole.

The tremors started once more.

"Hurry, Wil. Forget the chest. Climb up here," Sarah said.

Wil had the rope tied around the chest. He quickly climbed up and they started tugging the chest up. Mitch joined in to help. The tremor was stronger than before. The hole was starting to close in.

"Forget it, Wil," Holloman hollered.

He and Wil continued pulling the chest up. As soon as the hole closed, they were able to pull the chest up and onto solid ground. Wil just lay down and stared up at the sky. "We did it."

"We sure did," Sarah said with a smile. "No one will ever believe this. Now the question is finding our way out of here. I've never been to this part of the park. We have to be ten to fifteen miles north of the falls."

"Right now, we'll set up some kind of camp and get some rest. Tomorrow we'll figure out where we are."

Chapter 29

Saturday was busy for the group. Santiago and Condor took them to two museums and the library.

"This is amazing," Alexis said while in the library. "I may start reading when we return home."

Javier smiled at her. "You don't like to read?"

"No, I don't. Kelsey is the reader of the group. She's always reading some kind of book."

Kelsey smiled. "I just enjoy it. Fiction, nonfiction, you name it."

"Do you enjoy reading historical books?" Javier asked.

"I do. I'm always interested in learning about the history of a country or a civilization."

"We have a couple of books you may be interested in." He pulled out one and handed it to Kelsey. "This one deals with the slums in Rio. The book showcases the 1964 military coup in Brazil. Supported by civilians, the action was carried out by armed forces. Many still remember it."

Kelsey read the back cover of the book. "Interesting. If I were here longer, I might have had time to read it."

"I can purchase it for you and send it to you," Javier said.

Kelsey took a deep breath. "I don't mean any disrespect, Mr. Condor, but when we do business, we don't take gifts. However, I may consider purchasing it myself."

He smiled. "I can understand. You are not like many businesspeople. Most take bribes."

Kelsey glanced at one of the *blocos* from her hotel room. There were thousands of people dressed up in different outfits and colorful head attire. Her cell phone vibrated. She smiled. It was Maddie. "What's up, sweetie?"

"I was thinking about what you were doing, and if you were having fun."

"It's an amazing culture. Just been watching what they call a *bloco* — basically a street party in preparation for their major Carnival event in February. They're dressed in so many different garbs. It's unbelievable what people wear. Our plane leaves first thing in the morning. I should be back in Rapid City late tomorrow."

There was silence on the other end.

"Are you okay, Maddie?"

Still silent. Tessa got on the phone. "Kelsey, Wil and the group are trapped inside a cave in Yosemite National Park, and we haven't heard from anyone on where they are."

"Oh no." She couldn't speak.

"I'm so sorry."

"That explains why he hasn't responded to my texts. I'll see what I can find out from my father and get back to you. I have to have faith in Wil, or our relationship will never work."

"He'll be back, but I just wanted to let you know what is happening."

"Thanks." She got off the phone and quickly dialed her father.

"Kelsey, you decided to talk to your father?"

"Do you know anything that happened in California?"

"Are you talking about Yosemite?"

"Yes, I am. What is going on?"

"The group found an entrance to the cave, but a few minutes into the cave, the earth shook and the cave was sealed. Emergency crews are doing what they can to find them. Nothing yet."

"Do they know if anyone is dead?"

"Nothing."

"Please keep me posted." Kelsey called Tessa back and explained to her what had happened.

"Oh my," she said. "Please keep me posted."

"I will."

Kelsey shut her cell phone and turned at the knock on the door. She hurried over and glanced through the keyhole. Kelsey didn't know the man. She opened the door slightly. He handed her an envelope. "Please read this and go home as soon as you can."

~

Wil's eyes popped open when the sun shot up. He glanced around at the others who were fast asleep. Wil sat up and scanned the area. He was right. They were north of the entrance. The problem was they were in a very mountainous area and would be difficult to find a way down. He got up and scouted around. Several minutes later he found a trail that may be feasible to travel. What to do with the chest? Wil started digging a hole near a rock that he would remember. It took him half an hour to dig the hole.

Wil turned to Sarah's voice. "Good idea burying it here. We surely can't carry it."

Holloman helped Wil drop the chest in the hole, and Sarah covered it with dirt. Wil put a marker over it so they could remember where it was when they came back.

"We could wait here for someone to find us?" Sarah said.

Wil shook his head. "Could be a few days. And Mitch needs medical attention. Holloman popped the leg in place, but I'm not sure if it's set correctly."

"He did what he could, Wil," Sarah said.

"I found a trail that I may be able to descend. Then I'll send help."
Wil grabbed a couple of pieces of wood and set Mitch's leg into them. He started what Wil estimated to be nine-thousand feet down the side of the mountain. They all stared down.

"It's going to be slow going," Mitch said.

Wil smiled. "Nothing better to do on a sunny day. Sit tight. I'll be back as soon as I can. I left water and protein bars."

Holloman touched his shoulder. "Get us the help we need."

Wil had rappelled two thousand feet down the mountain by noon. When he took a break, Delilah, who was feeling much better and had also rappelled down, sat down by him. "This past week I'll never forget as long as I live. Thank you for coming to rescue us."

"I just happened to be there with you, and we were able to find a way out."

She laughed. "If you didn't, we may still be down there in that cave, our bones joining the others."

"Why did you become a research assistant?"

"Dr. Reynolds recruited me. I love the thought of finding out about our history and how it can help us in the future."

"Well, I feel the same way. I spend almost all of my time outdoors and enjoy it immensely."

"I can imagine."

Wil stood up. "Let's try to get down some more."

They glanced up as a chopper flew over them. They waved and shouted until the helicopter hovered over them. Just like that a man slid down on a rope.

"Are you all okay?"

"We're hurting, but we'll make it," Delilah said.

The man looked over at the others. "You must be Wil Bolton?"

Wil nodded.

"Wil, do you know of a place we can land safely and carry you all out of here?"

"On top of the mountain. That's where the others are."

He wrapped a rope around Delilah and pulled the rope. "Please, call Dr. Reynolds' father and let him know she's okay. He's been worried sick." When he pulled on the rope, they pulled her up. Wil was next. Once on the chopper, Wil showed them where the others were. They landed.

The man who had come down to save them helped

Wil load the chest onto the chopper.

"Wow, so Dr. Reynolds found what she was looking for."

"And more." She smiled at Wil. "We're taking you all to Mammoth Hospital in Mammoth Springs to get checked over."

"Thank you," Wil said.

"No problem. Glad we could assist here. There are a lot of people praying for this group. It's amazing what has happened. No one expected to find you. That area has seen four vanishings, and none of the victims have been found."

"We found their bones," Sarah said.

The guy's mouth stood agape. "Where?"

"In a cave with a lot of bones from over the years. Close to the treasure."

"Dr. Reynolds, the media is on this already. They're considering this one of the biggest finds in recent years in California."

She smiled. "This is so exciting."

Wil listened to the conversation. She didn't mention any of her assistants or other professors who had helped. It was all about her. He lay back and closed his eyes as the chopper flew toward the hospital. Thirty minutes later the chopper landed on the roof of the hospital. A stretcher was waiting for Mitch to take him into a room to have his leg checked. He heard the paramedics were taking the women and the other two to different examination rooms.

Chapter 30

Kelsey still hadn't opened the envelope she'd received last night, but now that she and the others were in the air, crossing over the Amazon en route to America, maybe she'd read it.

An hour into the flight, Kelsey climbed out of her seat and headed to the area where others were sitting and having a few drinks.

"Want something to drink, Kelsey?" Alexis asked.

"Water's fine."

Alexis locked eyes with her. "Are you pregnant?"

"Why would you ask that?"

"You haven't had alcohol in …I don't know how long."

"Water's fine." She grabbed a glass of water and joined them.

"What did you think?" Randolph asked.

Kelsey sipped her water before speaking. "Something is running through my mind, and I can't figure it out. How did Dr. Condor know about the new business venture?"

"Kelsey, it's not like it's a state secret," Alexis said.

Kelsey eyed her. "Brazil?"

Randolph glanced up. "You haven't seen this, have you?"

Kelsey took a Brazilian magazine from him. The front cover showed her dancing with Javier in the nightclub. The caption read, "What does her fiancé think? Is Kelsey Lawrence getting out of hand?" She laughed. "Where do they come up with these things?"

JJ looked at the magazine over her shoulder. "How will your fiancé react to it?"

Kelsey peered at him. "Nolan and I are no more. Back to our weekend. Thoughts, anyone?"

Gemini spoke first. "The sites are magnificent. However, I don't like the idea that they're being paid so poorly, but Mr. Santiago said they're working to increase the wages. So that's something."

"Anyone else?"

JJ jumped in. "I think the guy is perfect. Santiago knows what the world is all about. He knows what people want."

"Yeah, in Rio," Randolph said. "What about the rest of the country?"

Kelsey thought for a moment. "We'll bring all the information to our board this week. Gemini, please set up a meeting for Monday afternoon?"

"Will do."

Kelsey climbed out of her chair and went back to the front. She finally opened the note.

Ms. Lawrence, please think carefully before you go into business with Santiago and Dr. Condor; especially watch out for Condor's son. Check into Dr. Condor's references. He claims to be an anthropologist and an archaeologist. There are rumors he was caught stealing spoils from a dig site in Brazil within the last year.

Kelsey slipped the letter back into the envelope and placed it into her bag. How could they have missed this if it was true? She'd talk to Gemini when she returned to Chicago. A few minutes later, she fell asleep. She woke up to the captain's voice that they would be landing at Rapid City's airport in fifteen minutes.

When she grabbed her gear at the baggage claim, there waiting for her were Tessa and the kids.

Maddie hurried over and hugged her. "I'm glad you're back. They found Wil, and he's going to be okay."

Her eyes filled with tears, and her lips quivered. "That's great news. Thanks for letting me know." Kelsey's hand went to her chest, and she said a quick thank you to God.

Jonathan stood and looked at her. He lifted his arms toward Kelsey. Maddie whispered to her. "He wants you to hold him."

Kelsey lifted him up, and the little guy wrapped his arms around her. "I'm glad you're home safe, Aunt Kelsey. I'm glad Uncle Wil is okay."

"So am I."

They drove back to Nemo, and the minute they were back, Kelsey tried to call Wil. Still no answer. "Damn it," she said, closing the phone. She glanced up at Tessa who was standing there.

"I know how you feel. It's tough not knowing anything. We're all glad you're back safely." Tessa handed Kelsey a beer, and the two sat down on the porch. Tessa gazed around the place. "This is so peaceful. The week I've been here I've had a chance to think and rethink what has happened in my life. It started way back when I first met Cliff. I thought I was in love, but now I wonder. He was handsome, but there were signs he was lazy from the start. We got married."

"How does anyone know what will happen?"

"True, but you would think you'd have an idea of what would make you happy. For instance, Wil and Lydia were very close, and of course he was crushed when she was killed in that car wreck. We all were, and it took time to heal."

"I can imagine. I've never been in a relationship where I've contemplated marriage or having children. It seemed all the guys were parasites who wanted either my money or … you know."

"Right, I can imagine because you have money and looks."

"Thank you. That changed one day when I walked out of a casino and saw Wil sitting on a street bench counting cobblestones on Deadwood's Main Street."

Tessa laughed. "That sounds like my little brother. He does some of the craziest things. When he was five, he climbed up into a tree to rescue a kitten. No one knows how he got up there, but he did. They both fell out of the tree, but neither was hurt. Of course, Dad yelled at him and grounded him for life. Wil has probably been grounded for life at least a dozen times."

They both laughed.

Tessa took Kelsey's hand. "You talk about love, and I have to tell you that Wil is deeply in love with you, but he is afraid he won't be enough for you because of his lack of money."

"He's told me that, but I don't know how to convince him I feel the same way he does. I even thought about selling my business to show him that money doesn't mean anything to me. Wil means everything to me."

"He'd hate for you to sell your business, and so would you because I can tell from the short time we've known each other that you love it."

"I do, but I love Wil more, and I could never say that before." Kelsey took a swig of her beer. "Our relationship has been different than any I've ever been in. There was no question I would have slept with Wil the first night we were together. It took us two weeks before that happened, and I'm so happy about that." She laughed. "In fact, when we were camping with Bailey and Laney, twice I fell into his arms and I kept saying in my head to him, 'Kiss me, you fool.' He didn't."

Tessa laughed. "Again, that's Wil."

"I keep telling him I'll wait a week to see how our relationship works out, but the truth is I don't plan on ever leaving him."

"Then tell him that. It'll go a long way to establish the foundation you two are building. Don't ever screw with him because you'll lose him forever. Mom and Dad sent him to Savage High School because they didn't want him competing with his brothers."

"He has brothers?"

"Delbert and Cole. Our family is pretty divided. Wil and I are close, but we're not close to the others. Mom and Dad chose the other two boys over Wil, but I stuck by Wil because after I was married, he was the only one I could talk to about my marriage, and as you can tell, my children love him. And Maddie thinks of you as an important person in her life."

"Maddie is a unique girl. She reminds me a lot of Wil."

"She does, but she's had Wil as a male figure not her father. Whenever Maddie was hurting, she would call Wil, or when we lived near him, she'd have me drive over to see him or even call him to come over to see her. Wil would always respond, and it pissed Cliff off immensely."

Kelsey stood up. "Needless to say, I believe I've found the perfect guy for me. I just need to do something about it. But for now I'm going to bed because I have a Skype conversation tomorrow about our trip." She started to turn into the cabin and stopped. "Tessa, thank you for being there for Wil. I promise I'll do the same for the rest of his life."

"I can tell."

Chapter 31

The first person Wil saw when he opened his eyes was Xavier Holloman.

"I was hoping to see a beautiful gal named Kelsey, but instead I get you."

Holloman laughed. "I'm the only one who was stupid enough to stay with you."

"How long have you been here?"

"For three days now. That's how long you've been sleeping. You were bitten by a wild animal, and at first they thought it was rabies, but that was cleared. They're not sure what happened, other than you were bit by something, but now you're clean."

"What happened to the treasure?"

"About as I expected. Dr. Reynolds took credit for the finding, and the money will go to Reynolds and Lawrence. Your friend Loe got screwed out of any money, but Loe had the last laugh."

"Why?"

"He reported Dr. Reynolds to some kind of higher-education board dealing with ethics, and she was suspended for five years. And most important, Loe has hired me to keep you out of trouble."

They both laughed.

"Yeah, right," Wil said. "What about your daughter?"

"About her. I'll have to tell her, but I don't know how she's going to handle it or if she'll even believe it."

"I'll help anyway I can."

Holloman's eyes lit up. "Could you talk to her for me?"

"I will as long as you promise to walk her down the aisle when we get married."

"You're going to ask my baby to marry you?"

"Yeah, but I don't know when."

"Hopefully, soon because I don't know how long I can keep you alive." Holloman grinned.

"I'll do better, Dad. Where are you staying?"

"I'm not sure yet."

"Why don't you join me in South Dakota? Kelsey wants me to add rooms to my cabin, so why not now? It'll give you a chance to be with your daughter."

Holloman was silent. "Why not? And I'll tell her about her being my daughter. You won't have to do that. But you should call her to let her know you're alive."

~

The next day as Kelsey was on Skype talking to Gemini, Kelsey took a deep breath. "When they completed their research on Santiago, was there any mention of smuggling drugs or anything illegal they were doing?"

"No. Santiago seemed to be a straight-up guy.

Why?”

“I received a letter before we left yesterday suggesting Dr. Condor was involved in smuggling cocaine through Brazilian ports. In addition, Dr. Condor is a fraud. He stole some dig finds in Brazil.”

“Wow. There was nothing untoward in our research. Do you want me to dig a little deeper?”

“I’m not too concerned about Condor because I won’t have any dealings with him, but I am concerned about Santiago and the bank president’s son. And yes, dig a little deeper into those two.”

“I’ll follow up on the Rio project.”

“Thanks.”

As soon as she was off the phone, it rang once more. It was Wil. She grabbed it. “Are you okay?”

“Yes, I’m just resting in a hospital. There was nothing wrong, but the doctor’s decided to keep us for a couple of days to check us over. I did get bit by something. Originally, they thought it was rabies, but I’m all cleared.”

“Did you find it?”

“We found a treasure and a Bigfoot skull, but your father took all the credit for it and got all the royalties—not Mr. Loe.”

“How did that happen?”

“Long story that I’ll tell you when I return.”

“Are you coming home soon?”

“Tomorrow.”

“Whew. I’ve been so worried about you because I couldn’t get ahold of you to find out if everything was okay. Tessa has helped me a lot to understand who you are. I miss you so much and, Wil, I keep telling you I’ll give it another week to see about our relationship. But now I don't plan on going anywhere because I'm in love with you and want to be with you forever."

"I feel the same way about you. See you tomorrow."

Maddie came into the room just as Kelsey got off. "Was that Uncle Wil?"

"It was. He's coming home tomorrow."

"It's about time. He's had us scared long enough."

Chapter 32

The nurse finished checking Wil's vitals. "You're good to go."

"Thanks, ma'am."

As soon as the nurse left, Boris Loe walked in. "Wil, I see you're doing well. I'm glad."

"What brings you here?"

"I made it a point to check on my employees. It seems Mitch ended up the worst of it with the busted leg, but it sounds like he'll be just fine. I plan on bringing him back to Chicago so he can work in the gallery. He can decide from there if he wants to join you in the field or stay at the gallery. Mitch seems to have taken a shine for Delilah.

"We found what we were looking for, but we lost it all," Wil said.

"Not necessarily. Xavier Holloman testified before a national artifacts board who had discovered the artifact and the treasure. Specifically, you, so that means it's our find, and the Lawrences are out of everything. The Bigfoot skull goes into my gallery, and they can have the treasure. It pissed Lawrence off because he wanted the skull." Boris grinned. "Hank said he'd settle for the treasure, but the Presidio where it was stolen from has prior claim to the treasure. He lost out on that also. Needless to say, it was a good day for Loe Enterprises and a bad day for the Lawrences." He took a deep breath. "One last thing. My jet will be taking you back to Rapid City in a little bit. I understand Xavier Holloman will join you."

Wil nodded. "He said you hired him."

"What do you think of that?"

Wil grinned. "He said it was to keep me out of trouble, and he did a good job of that in Yosemite."

"Good. Get better quick because in a couple of weeks we'll be heading to some Pacific Ocean islands to search for another treasure. This one is underwater, not under a cave."

"Great."

Wil and Holloman landed at the Rapid City airport later that afternoon. Once there they grabbed their gear and headed to the pickup truck. An hour later, they arrived at the cabin in Nemo. As Wil parked the truck, Maddie and Jonathan came bursting out of the cabin.

"Are you okay?" Maddie said. "You should really find a way to contact us because we were worried not knowing where you were."

Wil picked her up and she hugged him.

"I'm just glad you're home."

He put her down and picked up Jonathan.

"I'm happy you're okay," the young boy said, hugging him.

Maddie looked up at the tall man in front of her.

"Who did you bring home with you, Uncle Wil?"

"This is Mr. Holloman. He's a good friend of the family and a great guy for you to get to know." Wil's eyes landed on Kelsey who was leaning against the post. He looked at the kids. "Your mom must be working."

"She is."

Wil turned to Kelsey and walked over to her.

Her head tilted to the side. "You made it home in one piece, and I told you I'd be waiting for you."

"You did, and I'm glad." He put his arms around her and kissed her gently on the lips. "We have a lot to talk about."

"We do."

"But first I have someone I'd like you to meet. And maybe you two should go for a walk up the trail to talk."

"Is he okay?"

Wil nodded. "He is. I'll be right here with the kids."

~

Holloman and Kelsey strolled up the trail just above the cabin. They both found a rock to sit on.

Kelsey started the conversation. "Wil said I needed to meet you. I know you're Xavier Holloman and you've worked for my father ever since I was born."

"I have but not anymore. I work with Mr. Loe and Wil with Treasure Paradise."

"What happened?"

"It's a long story that Wil will tell you someday. But what I have to tell you concerns you and me. I was in the Navy Seals for four years, and when I got out, your father hired me about twenty-six years ago to protect his family. When you were born, he specifically told me to protect you." He took a deep breath. "This is going to be hard, and I don't know if you'll believe me."

Kelsey waited for him to continue.

"I was at a bar one night, and your mother happened to be there. We both were drunk, and to make a long story short, we spent the night in a hotel room. Nine months later you were born."

"Are you saying you're my father?"

"I am. I know it may be hard for you to believe, but I am your father."

She blew out a breath and shook her head. "It's not hard to believe because I'm nothing like my dad, and I do know my mom has slept around. But if it's true, what proof do you have?"

"Nothing other than my word."

Kelsey stood up. "Does Wil know about this?"

"He does."

"And how does he feel about it?"

"You'll have to ask him. All he said was I needed to tell you the truth, so that's what I'm doing."

"You have, but please let me process all of this. My family has always done some rotten things, but I'm not sure about this." Kelsey strode down the hill to the cabin, peered up at Wil who sat on the porch.

"Do you believe him?"

"I don't know what to think."

Chapter 33

The next morning when Wil came out of the bedroom, he noticed Holloman hadn't slept on the couch. Tessa had slept with her children in one bedroom and Will and Kelsey were in another bedroom, leaving Holloman on the couch. Then Wil noticed the note on the stand next to the couch. He opened it.

Mr. Loe called me early this morning and wants me back in Chicago. He is sending the corporate jet to pick me up, and I called a taxi so I didn't have to wake anyone in the house. Thanks for the opportunity to meet my daughter. Until we meet again. Xavier Holloman.

Wil folded the letter and stuffed it in his pocket. Something just didn't seem right about the scenario. What was the purpose of it? He snapped his fingers and started looking around the cabin and found what he was looking for. A listening device.

When he was done searching around the house, he found three listening devices in the outer room and one in the bedroom he was sleeping in with Kelsey. He was sure there was another one in the other bedroom. Wil stepped outside and called Boris Loe who answered on the first ring.

"Wil, are you back in South Dakota?"

"I am. Holloman was here last night and just disappeared this morning. Did you call him back to Chicago?"

"I did not. He asked to stay there with you."

"He left a message saying you called him back. Something doesn't feel right here because before he left, he also installed several listening devices in the cabin."

"Why would he do something like that?"

"I have my thoughts but will keep them to myself until I'm sure."

Boris sighed at the other end. "It's safe to say I've been duped, and the guy is still working for Lawrence."

"Could you do me a favor and see if there is any possibility he is Kelsey's father?"

Boris laughed. "He mentioned that to me once before, and I dug into it. Hank Lawrence is Kelsey's father, and her mother is her mother. I have no clue what he's up to, but I'll dig into his background and see what I can find out. "On another note, our next treasure hunt is delayed until March or April because of permits we need to obtain and the weather. It seems like those two months are the best for searching because there aren't any tourists around, and the weather is much milder. I will be sending you documents associated with the next assignment."

"Sounds good." He sat down in the porch rocking chair.

"Any thoughts on how to handle the listening devices in the cabin?"

Wil was silent on his end. "We really don't talk about anything of significance in the cabin, but I'll talk to Kelsey about it and see what she has to say."

"Do you believe it has something to do with her business?"

"I'm not sure, but once I find out I'll do something about it."

"No, Wil, you're my employee now, and I want you focused on the work at hand. If you have any thoughts on it, I'll take care of it from this end. I have the money and the resources."

Once Wil got off the phone, he turned to see Kelsey standing in the doorway with a robe on. "I was wondering where you had gone. Is everything okay?"

"I was just talking to Boris about Holloman. I received a note saying that Boris called him back to Chicago."

Kelsey stepped out onto the porch. "It wasn't true, was it?"

Wil shook his head no.

"I've been thinking about it, and the guy is not my father. Despite who he is, Hank Lawrence is my father."

"It seems so."

"Then what's it all about?"

"I have my theories, but we can't talk about it here or right now."

"What's wrong?"

"I'll tell you, but let's get some breakfast and help my sister move into her new place."

Kelsey strolled over to Will and climbed on his lap.

"I'm not going back to Chicago because I'm to stay right here with you and run my business out of the cabin."

"Is that your final answer?"

"Now you're quoting from a game show. Wow, you are talented, but yes, love of mine, it's my final answer."

He planted a solid kiss, and she responded in kind.

A voice sounded behind them. "Yuk, I'm glad I have a long time before I meet a guy."

They both turned to Maddie and laughed. "I would hope so," Wil said.

Maddie ran over and jumped on their laps. "We're going to our new place this morning so you two can have your own privacy; at least that's what Mom told us. I think it's because she's tired of sleeping in bed with two kids."

Wil rolled his eyes. "She did it one night. It's probably because she doesn't want to stay in a rundown cabin when she can live in a nice three-bedroom house."

"That's probably true. Personally, I'd rather stay out here with you two."

Wil rubbed her hair. "Your mom knows you can stay out here anytime you want." He jumped up and lifted the young girl over his shoulder. "Let's go make some breakfast."

"What are we having?" she said, giggling as he carried her into the cabin.

"What do you want?"

"Pancakes."

"Pancakes it is."

~

Wil and Kelsey helped Tessa and the kids carry their belongings into their new house on Williams Street above Deadwood's Main Street. The house was right next to a church, and in the winter, Tessa could walk one block to the bank if she needed to. And more importantly the elementary school was one block away.

Once they were finished moving in her things, Tessa suggested they all head to a place called Lee Street Station Cafe where they grabbed sandwiches, chips, and drinks.

"Thanks for this," Kelsey said.

"You're welcome," Tessa said. "Thank you two for helping us through all of this. You two can return to building a relationship, something I know you two are trying to do."

"We're getting there," Wil said.

"I see that," Tessa agreed.

Wil finished sipping his coke. "Do you need any help buying furniture or anything else for the house — maybe a housewarming gift?"

Tessa thought about it. "It would be nice to have one of those layaway couches."

"Consider it done," Wil said.

"What about us?" Maddie asked.

Kelsey grinned. "What do you want, sweetie?"

"I want you two to get married."

Kelsey peered up into Wil's eyes. Then she turned back to Maddie. "Someday it will happen, I promise you."

"Good," Maddie said, munching on a chip.

An hour later Wil and Kelsey drove back toward Nemo. "What are we going to do now that the cabin is all ours?" Kelsey said.

He grinned. "I'm sure we can think of something."

She kissed him on the cheek. "I know exactly what we're going to do, but first you and I need to talk about Holloman."

"Yeah, I'm guessing he's not your father."

"No way is he my father, but I don't know what his game is."

"This is my theory, and remember it's just a theory, but do you remember anything being said about Holloman in Brazil?"

Kelsey thought for a moment. "No, I don't, but I did receive that note about a couple of others."

"Okay, just hear me out. What if the reason the group wants to be part of your clothing company is because it'll help them transport drugs in the clothing? Maybe it's happening right now, but of course you don't know because it's happening overseas. Holloman has planted all kinds of listening devices in the cabin. Maybe he planted them because you'll be working out of the cabin to do your business, and he'll have firsthand information for your father who hopes to take over the company to continue his business." Wil swallowed slowly. "And Loe said he knew where the drugs and money were, and that was why his brother was shot along that trail."

"Do you believe that?" Kelsey asked.

"It's something to think about, and if it's okay with you, I'll pass my theory on to Mr. Loe so he can follow up on it."

"What about the listening devices?"

"I'll just rip them out. I plan on redoing your office, that is if those are still your plans."

"Can you pull over somewhere?"

He did that. "Are you okay?"

She shifted her body so she could place her hands around his neck and peer into his eyes. "I made Maddie a promise that the two of us will be married someday, and we'll never break our promises from this day forward." She took a deep breath. "I was scared to death when guns were waved in my face, when you tried to escape a fire, and when I found out you had been buried in a cave. At one point, I thought about just going back home, but my heart wouldn't allow it. My heart belongs to you."

He kissed the tip of her nose.

She continued. "Guys usually try to sleep with me after a first date, but it took you two weeks to even kiss me. Why is that?"

Wil peered into her eyes. "I want more than that. I want to build a strong foundation for our future. I want to know that you will be home when I come back from traveling. I want you to hold me tight when I'm hurting. I want to have a children with you, but I also know that we have our whole life ahead of us to do all that."

Kelsey kissed him gently on the forehead. "I've cooked, cleaned, laughed, and blushed more than I ever have with any guy. It's safe to say you're the one."

"Does that mean you're staying?"

Kelsey laughed. "I told you once I climbed into your bed, I'll never be leaving it."

"I guess that would be a yes."

Chapter 34

Later that afternoon as shadows settled over the cabin, they took a walk up the trail before they returned for dinner. Wil fired up the grill and Kelsey came out with some burgers, potato salad, and drinks.

Once the burgers were ready, the two sat on the porch lost in their own thoughts. Kelsey turned to Wil. "I really love being out here with you. It's our perfect world."

"It is."

A rustling and a quick movement by the trees nearby made her catch her breath. "What was that?"

"What did you see?"

"I thought I saw something or somebody flash by us over there."

"The sun setting can cause that sometimes because of the shadows."

He pulled her up and they hurried into the cabin. As Wil shut the door, someone knocked Wil to the ground. A man jumped on top of him and grabbed Wil around his throat.

Kelsey screamed then searched for something. Anything to be a weapon. She grabbed a big frying pan beside the stove. She grabbed it and started slamming the guy on the head. "Get the hell away from Wil." She must have hit him half a dozen times before the intruder finally fell off. He was out. Kelsey dropped the frying pan and fell to her knees beside Wil. "Are you okay?"

His eyes were closed, and he didn't respond.

"Open your eyes!" Kelsey started to give Wil mouth-to-mouth resuscitation.

In moments that seemed like minutes, he opened his eyes and winked at her.

"You asshole."

"Thanks for saving me."

"Who is that guy?" She pointed at the body lying a few feet away.

"Sebastian Peak. otherwise known as the Bigfoot of the Black Hills. He's believed to have raped several women in the Black Hills. Please get some rope. I'll tie him up and call the sheriff."

Kelsey hurried to the closet, grabbed the rope, and returned.

Wil tied him tightly before he woke up. He made sure he was secure and called the sheriff. "Hey, Sheriff, we have Sebastian Peak here gift wrapped and waiting for you."

"Wow. You expect us to come out there after dark?"

Wil laughed. "Your choice. We can keep him here until morning."

"No, we'll come and get him. How was your time with that sexy Chicago doll?"

Wil laughed to himself. He handed the radio phone to Kelsey. "The sexy Chicago doll has enjoyed every moment in the Black Hills."

"I'm so sorry, Kelsey. I thought you had left."

Kelsey laughed. "It's okay. Wil has shown me a good time. I knocked this big dude out with a frying pan."

"A frying pan?"

"He was trying to strangle Wil. I wasn't about to let that happen because I'm the only one who gets that pleasure."

The sheriff laughed.

It was around eleven when a deputy picked up Sebastian Peak. Finally, Wil climbed into bed where Kelsey was waiting for him. "What's this? All your clothes are still on."

"Not tonight, Wil. That man scared me. I'm going to stick as close as I can to you."

Wil fell asleep quickly. Kelsey continued staring around the room making sure nothing was happening. She climbed out of bed and double-checked the door. Wil had fixed it, and it felt sturdy. It was around three when she finally fell asleep.

Kesley's head popped up when the rooster crowed. She glanced around and fell back to sleep until nine when she woke up and saw that Wil was still sleeping. *He always seems to sleep peacefully.* Kelsey crawled into the shower and shivered at the cold water, then came out with a towel wrapped around her body. She finished drying her hair, which was getting much too long. She actually liked her hair this way.

She returned to the bedroom and sat on the side of the bed, gently stroking Wil's hair. A few moments later, he opened his eyes. Kelsey smiled at him. "Wake up, sleeping beauty. What are we going to do today?"

"Well for starters—" he pulled off her towel, pulled down his bedspread, and lifted her on top of him.

"Wil, I just took a shower. Oh hell, I can always take another one."

It was around ten when the two were sitting at the table eating scrambled eggs and toast. They both jumped up as the door opened. Kelsey quickly slid out of sight.

"Wil Bolton."

"Good morning, Silas."

"Where's my brother?"

"As far as I know, he's with the sheriff, probably in county lockup."

"And why…"

Kelsey came up from behind and smacked the man alongside the head with the skillet.

Wil frowned. "What did you just do?"

She shrugged. "It worked for the bigger man."

"You shouldn't have done that, Kelsey. Let's get out of here. When he wakes up, he'll be one pissed-off person."

When Wil headed toward the front door, she said, "Not that way. Out through the back door."

Wil grabbed their jackets and followed her into the forest, but she was fast. She was waiting for him with her arms crossed. "What was that all about?"

"I may have forgotten to mention that Sebastian had an older brother. In fact, three brothers. And they all live close."

"What the hell are you thinking, Wil?"

"Here put your jacket on. You'll need it where

we're going."

"Where are we going?"

"To the Nemo Guest Ranch Store."

"I thought you were supposed to protect me. I thought it would be safe here with you."

"Damn it, Kelsey I'm doing the best I can."

"Don't yell at me, Wil. I've had a gun poked in my face, waited for you to escape a fire, and found out you were buried in a cave. I don't want to be your next catastrophe."

"You've already mentioned that. Do you really believe you'll be my next catastrophe?"

"No. I'm sorry, but I'm scared. When I'm scared, I ramble on and say irrelevant things."

Wil stared at her. "We'll get out of this."

"If we do, you and I are going to be married. Especially since I may be carrying your child."

He stared at her.

She grimaced. "Probably irrelevant information right now."

Wil pointed. "Run. That way. Fast."

THE END

Other books by this author

Bouncing Back

The Battle Off the Court

Success on the Hard Wood

Tragedy Off the Court

Freedom Flight

Fight for Survival

Road to Hell

A New Life Begins

Relentless

Missing

Targeted

Author Bio: My wife, Susan and I have two sons, Justin (Kayla) and Jeremy and a grandson, Aiden. Born and raised in South Dakota. I enjoy spending time with family, traveling and putt-putt. I recently retired as managing editor of a small town Iowa newspaper. I am a former Marine Corps veteran, getting my start in the publishing business in

1981 working for several years on base newspapers. I spent time running my own freelance business. I love writing. I enjoy reading anything and everything. I also love the history of our country and enjoy reading western books, mysteries, and adventure novels, and watching mystery, adventure, and western movies.